Sheriff Carter Jackson felt his breath catch in his throat as he started down into the ravine.

He raised his binoculars and felt his heart lift like helium. Eve Bailey rose from where she'd been hidden in the rocks.

"I've found her," he said into the two-way radio. "Bring the horse to the top of the ravine." Carter dismounted and, taking his pack with his rescue gear, started down the rocky slope.

As he cut off her ascent, he realized he was nervous about seeing Eve. This was crazy. It had been years. She'd probably forgotten that night in the front seat of his old pickup behind her parents' barn.

Just then she looked up and he knew Eve hadn't forgotten—or forgiven him.

B.J. DANIELS

SECRET OF DEADMAN'S COULEE

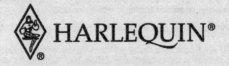

HARLEQUIN®

TORONTO • NEW YORK • LONDON
AMSTERDAM • PARIS • SYDNEY • HAMBURG
STOCKHOLM • ATHENS • TOKYO • MILAN • MADRID
PRAGUE • WARSAW • BUDAPEST • AUCKLAND

This is for Rob Myers, former coroner and always a mystery lover. Thanks, Rob, for all your help over the years. You are one of the few people I can call and ask about dead bodies, poisons and cool scary stuff.

ISBN-13: 978-0-373-88770-5
ISBN-10:   0-373-88770-1

SECRET OF DEADMAN'S COULEE

Copyright © 2007 by Barbara Heinlein

www.eHarlequin.com

Printed in U.S.A.

ABOUT THE AUTHOR

B.J. Daniels's life dream was to write books. After a career as an award-winning newspaper journalist, she sold thirty-seven short stories before she finally wrote her first book. That book, *Odd Man Out*, received a 4½ starred review from *Romantic Times BOOKreviews* and went on to be nominated for Best Harlequin Intrigue of 1995. Since then she has won numerous awards, including a career achievement award for romantic suspense.

B.J. lives in Montana with her husband, Parker, two springer spaniels, Spot and Jem, and an aging, temperamental tomcat named Jeff. When she isn't writing, she snowboards, camps, boats and plays tennis.

To contact B.J., write to her at P.O. Box 1173, Malta, MT 59538, e-mail her at bjdaniels@mtintouch.com or check out her Web site at www.bjdaniels.com.

Books by B.J. Daniels

CAST OF CHARACTERS

Sheriff Carter Jackson—Fate had given him another chance with the woman he wanted more than anything. Now if he could just keep her alive.

Eve Bailey—She was determined to learn the truth about herself—and what she'd found in a ravine south of her ranch.

Lila Bailey—She'd lived with more lies than anyone should have to.

Loren Jackson—He'd lost the woman he loved once, and he wasn't going to do it again.

Bridger Duvall—What was this mystery man doing in Whitehorse?

Arlene Evans—The town gossip was clueless about what was really going on. Or was she?

Nina Mae Cross—She'd lost more than her mind. She'd lost the man she loved.

Errol Wilson—He had his reasons for being bitter.

Deena Turner Jackson—She wanted what she couldn't have and she would do anything to get it.

Chapter One

A grouse burst from the sagebrush in an explosion of wings. Eve Bailey brought her horse up short, heart jammed in her throat and, for the first time, was aware of just how far she'd ridden from the ranch.

The wind had kicked up, the horizon to the west dark with thunderheads. She could smell the rain in the air.

She'd ridden into the badlands, leaving behind the prairie with its deep grasses to ride through sage and cactus, to find herself in no-man's-land with a storm coming.

Below her lay a deep gorge the Missouri River had carved centuries ago through the harsh eastern Montana landscape. Erosion had left hundreds of ravines in the unstable soil, and the country was now badlands for miles, without a road, let alone another person in sight.

Eve stared at the unforgiving land, her heart just as desolate. She should never have come home.

The wind whirled dust around her, the horizon blackening with clouds that now swept toward her.

She had to turn back. She'd been foolish to ride this far out so late in the day, let alone with a storm coming.

Even if she took off now she would never reach the ranch before the weather hit. Yet she still didn't move.

She couldn't get the image of what she'd seen out of her mind. Her mother and another man. She felt sick at the memory of the man she'd seen leaving her mother's house by the back door.

She shivered. The temperature was dropping rapidly. She had to turn back now. She'd been so upset that she'd ridden off dressed only in jeans and a T-shirt, and there was no shelter between here and the ranch.

A storm this time of year could be deadly for anyone without shelter. Turning her horse, she bent her head against the wind as the rainstorm moved in.

A low moan filled the air. She brought her horse up short again and listened. Another low, agonizing moan rose on the wind. She turned back to listen. The sound seemed to be coming from the ravine below her.

A gust of wind kicked up dust, whirling it around her. She bent her head against the grit that burned her eyes as she swung down from her horse and stepped to the edge of the steep ravine.

Shielding her eyes, she peered down. Far below, along a wide rocky ledge, stood a thick stand of giant junipers. As the wind whipped down the steep slope, the branches parted and—

There was something there, deep in the trees. She saw the glint of metal in the dull light and what could have been a scrap of clothing.

Goose bumps rose on her arms as she heard the low moan again. *Someone* was down there.

The first few drops of rain slashed down, cold and wet as they soaked instantly into her clothing. She barely noticed as the air filled with another moan. She caught sight of movement. From behind the thick nest of junipers, a scrap of faded red fabric flapped in the wind.

"Hello!" she called, the wind picking up

her words and hurling them across the wide ravine.

No answer.

Common sense told her to head toward the ranch before the weather got any worse. Eve Bailey was no stranger to the risk of living in such an isolated, unpopulated part of the state. She'd been born and raised only miles from here. She knew how quickly a storm could come in.

This part of Montana was famous for extreme temperature changes that could occur from within hours to a matter of minutes. It was hard country in which to survive. Five generations of Baileys would attest to that.

But if there was someone down there, someone injured, she couldn't just leave them.

"Hello!" she called again, and was answered by that same low, agonizing moan. Below her, the scrap of red cloth fluttered in the wind and, beside it, what definitely appeared to be metal glittered. *What* was down there?

A gust of wind howled past, and another low moan rose from the trees. She glanced back at the ominous clouds, then down into the vertical-sided ravine as she debated what to do.

She was going to have to go down there—and on foot. It was one thing to risk her own neck, but there was no way she was going to risk her horse's.

The ravine was a sheer drop at the top, widening as it fell to the ledge and growing steeper again as it dropped to the old riverbed far below. This end of Fort Peck Reservoir was dry from years of drought, the water having receded miles down this canyon.

Across the chasm the mountains were dark with pines. This side was nothing but eroded earth and a few stands of wind-warped junipers hanging on for dear life.

Eve loosely tied her horse to a tall sage. If she didn't get back before the storm hit, she didn't want her mare being struck by lightning. Better to let the horse get to lower ground just in case, even though it meant she'd have to find the mare to get home.

From experience she knew the soil into the ravine would be soft and unstable. But she hadn't expected it to give under her weight the way it did. The top layer of dirt and shale began to avalanche downward, taking it with her from her first step off.

She slid, descending too fast, first on her feet, then on her jean-clad bottom. She dug in her heels, but it didn't slow her down, let alone stop her. As she barreled toward the ledge, she realized with growing concern that if the junipers didn't stop her, then she was headed for the bottom of the ravine.

The eerie sound again filled the air. The wind and rain chilled her to the bone as she slid at breakneck speed toward the sound. She swept past an outcropping of rock and grabbed hold of a jutting rock. But she couldn't hold on.

The rough rock scraped off her skin, now painful and bleeding, but the attempt had slowed her down a little. Now if the junipers would just stop her—

That's when she saw the break in the rock ledge. While the ledge ran across the ravine, a part of it had slid out and was now funnel shaped. Eve was heading right for the break in the rocks.

Just before the ledge, she grabbed for the thickest juniper limb she could reach and hung on. The bark tore off more skin from her already bloody palm as her hand slid along it and finally caught. The pain was excruciating.

Worse, her momentum swung her around the branch and smacked her hard into another thick trunk, but she was finally stopped. She took a ragged breath, exhaling on a sob of pain, relief and fear as she crouched on the ledge and tried to get herself under control.

Trembling from the cold and the fall down the ravine, she pulled herself up by one of the branches. She'd banged her ankle on a loose rock at the base of the junipers. It ached, but she was just thankful that it wasn't broken as she stood, clinging to the branch, and looked down.

She'd never liked heights. She swayed, sick to her stomach as she saw how the ground dropped vertically to a huge pile of rocks in the river bottom far below.

Her legs were trembling, her body aching, hands bleeding and scraped, but her feet were on solid ground.

A jagged flash of lightning split the sky overhead, followed quickly by a reverberating boom of thunder.

Through the now-pouring rain, Eve looked back up the steep slope she'd just plunged down. No chance of getting out that way. She felt sick to her stomach because she had no idea how she was going to get herself out of here, let alone anyone else.

"Hello?" she called out.

No answer.

"Is anyone down here?" she called again.

She listened. Nothing but the sound of the rain on the rocks at her feet.

She couldn't see the scrap of red cloth. Nor whatever had appeared to glint like metal from the top of the ravine. The junipers grew so thick she couldn't see into them or around them. Nor was she sure she could get past them the way they crowded the ledge.

The wind howled down the ravine as the sky darkened and the brunt of the storm settled in, the rain turning to sleet. From deep in the trees came the eerie low moan.

Chilled to the bone, Eve edged along the rock ledge, clinging to branches to keep from falling as she moved toward the sound. The sleet fell harder, the wind blowing it horizontally across the ravine.

She hadn't gone but a few yards when she heard a faint flapping sound—the cloth she'd seen from the top of the ravine! She moved toward the sound and saw the strap of faded red fabric, the edges frayed and ragged. Past the cloth, dented and dusty metal gleamed dully in the cloud-obscured light.

Her mouth went dry, her pulse its own thunder in her ears, as she saw what was left of a small single-engine airplane. With a shock, she realized the crashed plane had to have been there for years. One wing was buried in the soft dirt of the ravine, the rest of the plane completely hidden by the junipers as if the trees had conspired to conceal it.

The moan startled her as the wind rushed over the weathered metal surface of the plane.

It had only been the wind.

She clung to a juniper branch as the storm increased in intensity, lightning slicing down through the canyon, thunder echoing in ear-splitting explosions over her head. Water streamed over the rock ledge, dark and slick with muddy soil.

She let out a sob of despair. She wouldn't be getting out of here anytime soon. Even if she could find a way off the rock ledge, it would be slippery now, the soil even more unstable.

Holding a branch back out of her way, she moved to the edge of the cockpit and used her sleeve to wipe the dirty wet film from the side of the glass canopy.

Cupping her hand over her eyes, she peered inside.

Eve reared back, flailing to keep from falling off the ledge, as her startled shriek echoed across the ravine.

She was shaking so hard she could hardly hold on to the juniper branch as rain and sleet thumped the canopy and the wind wailed over what was left of the plane.

She closed her eyes, fighting to erase the image from her mind, the macabre scene inside the plane chilling her more than the storm.

The pilot's seat was empty, and the strip of torn red cloth caught in the canopy was now flapping in the growing wind. The seat next to it was also empty, but there was a dark stain on the fabric.

The passenger in the back hadn't been so lucky. Time and the elements had turned the corpse to little more than a mummified skeleton, the dried skin shrunken down over the facial bones, the eyes hollow sockets staring out at her.

Not even that was as shocking as what she'd seen sticking out of the corpse's chest—the handle of a hunting knife, grayed from the years, the blade wedged between the dead man's ribs.

Chapter Two

Sheriff Carter Jackson had a theory about bad luck. He'd decided that some men attracted it like stink on a dog. At least that had been the case with him.

His luck had gone straight south the day he found Deena Turner curled up and waiting for him in his bed. He'd been more than flattered. Hell, Deena had been the most popular girl in high school, sexy and beautiful, the girl every red-blooded male in Whitehorse, Montana, wanted to find waiting for him in his bed.

So Carter had done what any dumb nineteen-year-old would do. He'd thanked his lucky stars, never suspecting that the woman was about to take him to hell and back.

Finding Deena in his bed had only been the beginning of a string of mistakes over the next twelve years that culminated in Deena lying about being pregnant and the two of them running off and getting married.

It had been hard at first to admit he'd made a mistake marrying her. He'd seen marriage as forever and divorce as failure. So he'd hung in. Right up until he caught Deena in bed with his best friend.

That had been two years ago. Since then he'd gone through a long, drawn-out, painful divorce. Painful because he felt guilty that it hurt more losing his best friend than it did ending it for good with Deena.

But that was the problem. It hadn't ended for good with Deena. Two weeks ago, she'd decided she wanted him back and that she would do anything to make that happen.

And she meant *anything.*

He pulled up in front of the house he and Deena had shared during their marriage. It was too early in the morning for this, but he just wanted to get it over with. Weighed down with dread, he climbed out of his patrol car, trying to remember a time when he'd looked forward to seeing Deena in the morning.

As he walked up the cracked sidewalk, he told himself this would be the last time. No matter what.

He grimaced at the thought, remembering how many times he'd left during their twelve years of marriage only to go back out of guilt or a sense of obligation. No wonder Deena just assumed he would always come back to her. He always had.

She opened the door to his knock almost as if she'd been expecting him. After what she'd left at his office for him, he didn't doubt she was.

She was wearing one of his old T-shirts and, from what he could tell, little else. His once-favorite scent floated around her. Her blond hair was pulled up, loose tendrils framing her pretty face.

"Hello, Carter," she said in that sultry voice, the one that had once been his undoing. "I had a feeling you'd be by this morning." She shoved open the door a little wider and gave him "the look." Boy, did he know *that* look.

Without a word, he reached into his pocket and took out the plain white envelope with her name and address neatly typed on it and handed it to her.

She took it, her smile slipping a little. "Something for *me?* You shouldn't have."

No, he thought, *you* shouldn't have. All the surprise visits at work and at his house, the presents, the constant phone calls, the urgent messages. The more he'd tried to get her to stop, the worse she had become.

He waited as she opened the envelope, resting his hand on the butt of the weapon at his hip.

Her eyes widened as she took out the legal form and read enough that, when she spoke, her sultry voice was long gone. "What the hell is this?"

"It's a restraining order. From this time forward you are not to contact me, send me any more letters or packages or come within one-hundred-and-fifty feet of me."

She narrowed her eyes at him. "We live in Whitehorse, Montana, you dumb bastard. The whole town is only a hundred and fifty feet long."

"If you break the restraining order you will be arrested," he said, hating that it had come to this.

He tipped his hat and turned his back to her as he headed for his vehicle, hoping she didn't have a gun, because he was pretty sure she'd have no compunction about shooting him in the back.

"You just made the biggest mistake of your life, Carter Jackson!" she yelled after him. "You're going to regret this as long as you live, you smug son of a bitch. If you think you can just walk away from me—"

The slamming of his patrol-car door thankfully cut off the rest of her words. This was not the morning to tempt him into arresting her for threatening an officer of the law.

It had taken him years, but he finally understood Deena. She only wanted what she couldn't have. His allure was that he hadn't been available. Just before he found her in his bed, he'd begun dating a neighboring ranch girl he'd known all his life, a girl he was getting serious with.

And that, he knew now, was why Deena had thrown herself at him. Deena had always been jealous of Eve Bailey and became worse after he and Deena married. Even the mention of Eve's name would set Deena off. He'd never understood her jealousy, especially since Eve had left the area right after high school and hadn't come back.

Until two weeks ago. Just about the time Deena decided she was going to get him back, come hell or high water.

As Carter drove away, he didn't look in his ex's direction, although out of the corner of his eye he saw that she'd come down the sidewalk in her bare feet and was now waving the restraining order and yelling obscenities at him.

"Good-bye, Deena," he said, hoping his luck was about to change. Maybe she would meet an unavailable long-haul trucker who'd take her far, far away.

As he drove back toward his office in the large three-story brick county courthouse, his radio squawked.

"Lila Bailey just called," the dispatcher told him. "She's worried about her daughter. Says they had a big storm down that way last night. Her daughter apparently went for a horseback ride yesterday evening and didn't return home last night."

"Which daughter?" Carter asked, his heart kicking up a beat.

"Eve Bailey."

The way his luck was going, of course it would be Eve. He'd grown up around the Bailey girls. Eve was hands-down the most headstrong of the three. And that was saying a lot. But she was also the most capable. She knew that country south of town. If anyone could survive a night out there, even in a bad storm, it was Eve.

"Lila said one of Eve's sisters saw her ride out yesterday evening toward the Breaks. Eve is staying in her grandmother's old house down the road from her folks' place so no one knew she hadn't returned until her horse came back this morning without her."

Carter rubbed the back of his neck. There was nothing south of the Bailey ranch but miles and miles of Missouri Breaks badlands. Searching for Eve would be like looking for a needle in a haystack. "Tell Lila I'm on my way."

IT WAS A SLOW NEWS DAY at the *Milk River Examiner* office. Glen Whitaker had come in early to work on a feature story he was writing about the couple who'd just bought the hardware store. This was news, since the population of the county had been dropping steadily for years now. While parts of Montana were growing like crazy, the towns along the Hi-Line were losing residents to more prosperous places.

Glen ran a hand over his buzz-cut blond hair and glanced out his office window past the park to the railroad tracks. A coal train was rumbling past. His phone rang. He let it ring a couple more times as he waited for the train to pass and the noise level to drop. "Hello."

"One of the Bailey girls is missing."

Glen groaned to himself as he recognized the voice of the worst gossip in the county.

From the moment he took the job as reporter at the *Milk River Examiner,* Arlene Evans had been feeding him information as if she was Deep Throat.

"Missing?" Most of Arlene's "leads" turned out to either be erroneous or the type of news he wasn't allowed to print. He'd ended up at Whitehorse after working for several larger papers where he'd made the mistake of printing things he shouldn't have.

He didn't want to lose his job over some small-town gossip. But then again, he had printer's ink in his veins. Working for a weekly newspaper, all he wrote about were church socials and town-council meetings.

Glen Whitaker was ready for a good story. "Which Bailey girl?"

"*Eve* Bailey. I just talked to Lila, her mother, and she said Eve rode out yesterday afternoon," Arlene said with her usual relish. "Her horse came back this morning without her."

Like the Baileys, Arlene lived south of Whitehorse.

The first settlement of Whitehorse had been nearer the Missouri River. But when the railroad came through, the town migrated five miles north, taking the name with it.

The original settlement of Whitehorse was

now little more than a ghost town except for a handful of ranches and a few of the original remaining buildings. It was locally referred to as Old Town.

The people who lived there were a close-knit bunch to the point of being clannish. They did for their own, seldom needing any help and definitely not interested in any publicity when something bad happened.

But this could turn out to be just the story Glen had been waiting for—if Eve Bailey didn't turn up alive and well.

Glen already had a headline in mind: Whitehorse Woman Lost In The Breaks, No Body Found.

"Her horse came back without her, so she's stranded out there?"

Arlene clucked her tongue, her voice dropping conspiratorially. "Little chance of surviving that storm on foot. No shelter out there. And it got really cold last night."

Whitehorse Woman's Body Found Frozen.

Unfortunately, it was June and while it could snow in the Breaks any month of the year, the chances were good she hadn't frozen to death. But hypothermia was a real possibility.

The problem was Glen knew about the Bailey girls, as they were called, although they were now young women. Attractive, but head-strong and capable. With his luck, Eve Bailey would survive. No heartrending story here.

He could picture Eve Bailey, so different from her sisters, who were blond with blue eyes. Eve had long dark hair and the blackest eyes he'd ever seen. But then he'd always been attracted to brunettes rather than blondes.

"Everyone is meeting over at the community center," Arlene was saying in her excited high voice. "The women are putting together a potluck for the search party. It's sewing day. We have to finish a quilt for Maddie Cavanaugh's engagement to my son. With Pearl in the hospital with pneumonia we're behind on the quilting. You know quilts are a tradition down here."

He groaned inwardly. "I know." Arlene had tried to get him to do a story on the White-horse Sewing Circle ever since he'd taken the reporter job. The group of women met most mornings at the community center and had for years. He suspected it was where Arlene picked up most of her gossip.

"I have to go. My pies are ready to come out of the oven," Arlene said.

"Are you making one of your coconut-custard pies?" Glen asked hopefully. Arlene had taken a blue ribbon last year at the Phillips County Fair with her coconut-custard pie—and he'd been one of the judges.

"I always make the coconut-custard when there's trouble," Arlene said. "This could be your biggest story of the year."

Arlene was forever hoping to be the source of his biggest story of the year. "My daughter Violet is helping me," she said, shifting gears. "Did I tell you she's quite the cook?"

Along with dispensing gossip, quilting and pie baking, Arlene Evans also worked at matchmaking, although she'd had little luck getting her thirty-something daughter, Violet, married off. From what Glen had heard Arlene had been trying to marry off Violet since she was a teenager.

The older Violet got, the more desperate Arlene had become. She considered it a flaw in her if her daughter was husbandless.

"Save me a piece of pie," he said as he grabbed his camera and notebook, figuring it would probably be a waste of gas, time and energy. He was sure that by the time he reached Whitehorse, Eve Bailey would have been found and there would be nothing more than a brief story about her harrowing night out in the storm.

For a piece of Arlene's coconut-custard pie he could even feign interest in her daughter.

BY THE TIME Sheriff Carter Jackson picked up his roping horse and trailer from his brother's place and reached the Old Town Whitehorse Community Center, there were a dozen pickups and horse trailers parked in front.

He pulled into the lot, noticing that all of the trucks and horse trailers were covered in the gray gumbo mud that made unpaved roads in this part of the state impassable after a rainstorm.

Fortunately, the sun had come out this morning and had dried at least the top layer of soil because it appeared everyone had made it.

He'd always been proud that he was from Old Town and was sorry his family was no longer part of this isolated community. No matter how they were getting along at the time, the residents pulled together when there was trouble like a large extended family.

As he pushed open the door of the community center, he spotted Titus Cavanaugh at the center of a group of men. Titus had a topographical map stretched out on one of the women's sewing tables and was going over it with the other male residents.

"Here's the sheriff now," resident Errol Wilson announced as Carter walked toward them.

"We're putting together a search party," said the elderly Cavanaugh, who was unmistakably in charge. If Old Town had been an incorporated town, Titus would have been mayor. He led the church services at the community center every Sunday, organized the Fourth of July picnic and somehow managed to be the most liked and respected man in the county, hell, most of the state.

His was one of the first families in the area. His grandmother had started the Whitehorse Sewing Circle and never missed a day until her death. Titus's wife Pearl was just as dedicated to the group, although Carter didn't see her. He'd heard Pearl was in the hospital with pneumonia. She'd always made sure that every newborn got a quilt, as well as every newlywed. It had been an Old Town tradition for as long as anyone could remember.

"Give me a minute," Carter said to Titus. "I'd like to talk to Eve's family before we head out."

He gathered the Bailey women in a small room at the back of the community center and closed the door. Lila Bailey was a tall, stern-looking woman with long gray-blond hair she kept in a knot at the nape of her neck. At one time, she'd been beautiful. There was still a ghost of that beauty in her face.

With her were her daughters, McKenna and Faith, both home from college. Chester Bailey, Lila's husband, was living in White-horse, working for the Dehy in Saco. Apparently, he hadn't arrived yet.

"Any idea where Eve was headed?" Carter asked. The women looked to McKenna, the second oldest Bailey sister.

"I was just coming home when I saw her ride out late yesterday afternoon," McKenna said, and glanced toward her mother.

Carter couldn't miss the look that passed between the two women. "Was that unusual for her? To take a horseback ride late in the afternoon with a storm coming in?"

"Eve is a strong-minded woman," Lila said. "More than capable of taking care of herself. Usually." The last word was said quietly as Lila looked to the floor.

"Where does she generally ride?" he asked the sisters.

Both shrugged. "Depending what kind of mood she's in, she rides toward the Breaks," McKenna said.

"What kind of mood was she in yesterday afternoon?" Carter asked, watching Lila's face.

Faith made a derisive sound. "Eve's often in a lousy mood." Lila shot her a warning look. "Well, it's true."

Faith and McKenna were in their early twenties. Eve was the oldest at thirty-two.

Lila apparently hadn't expected to have any more children after Eve. Both McKenna and Faith had been surprises—at least according to Old Whitehorse gossip. The local scuttle-butt was that Lila's husband, Chester, had been heartbroken they'd never had a son and their marriage strained to the point of breaking.

But Chester had only recently moved out of the house, taking a job in Saco. While as far as Carter knew the couple was still married, word was that Chester hardly ever came home. His daughters visited him up in Whitehorse.

One of the joys of small-town living: everyone knew everyone else's business, Carter thought.

"You should tell him," McKenna said to her mother in a hushed whisper.

The look Lila gave her daughter could have cut glass. "He's not interested in family matters, McKenna."

"On the contrary, I'm interested in Eve's

state of mind when she took off yesterday," Carter said, looking from McKenna to her mother.

"It was nothing," Lila said. "Just a disagreement. Why are we standing around talking? Eve could be injured. You should be out looking for her." She shot Carter a look that said she wasn't saying anything more about her disagreement with her oldest daughter. "Now if you'll excuse me I have to see to the potluck. Everything needs to be ready for when the men return with my daughter."

She left the room, Faith looking after her, plainly curious about what was going on between her mother and sister.

"If you wouldn't mind," Carter said. "I'd like a word with McKenna alone."

Faith shrugged and left, but with obvious reluctance. When the door closed behind her, Carter asked McKenna, "Why don't you tell me about the disagreement your mother and sister had yesterday and let me decide if it's relevant."

"You mean what they were arguing about? I don't know. I heard them yelling at each other when I came home. Eve stormed out to the barn, riding off a few minutes later. When

I asked Mother what was going on, she said it was just Eve being dramatic."

He'd seen Eve angry on more than one occasion, but he'd never thought of her as the dramatic type. Deena on the other hand... "The last time you saw your sister, how was she dressed?"

McKenna shrugged. "Jeans, boots, a T-shirt. I don't think she took a jacket. It was pretty hot when she left."

"What color T-shirt?" he asked, attempting to keep his growing concern from his voice. Eve hadn't been dressed for a night out in the weather—especially last night with that storm that had blown through. For some reason, she'd taken off upset, without even a jacket, and that alone he knew could have cost her her life.

"Light blue T-shirt," McKenna said, sounding close to tears as if realizing that her sister might be in serious trouble.

"Don't worry, we'll find her," Carter said, shocked to think that after all these years he would be seeing Eve Bailey again. He just hoped to hell he'd find her alive. But as he joined the search party, he feared they were now looking for a body.

Chapter Three

Lila Bailey busied herself arranging the food as it arrived from local residents. She had to keep busy or she knew she would lose her mind. The thought shook her, considering that her mother, Nina Mae, had literally lost hers and was now in the nursing home in Whitehorse.

The only way Lila could cope was not to allow herself even the thought that her oldest daughter wasn't coming back. Eve could take care of herself. Eve was the strong one. Eve was a survivor. Even as upset as she'd been yesterday.

Lila had to believe that. If she gave in to doubts, she knew she wouldn't be able to hold herself together and for Lila, losing control had always been her greatest fear.

More food arrived. She arranged it on the

extra tables the men had set up for her. Everyone pitched in when needed. She recalled with shame how the town had offered help when they heard Chester had left her.

Her face flamed at the pity she'd seen in their faces. No one believed Chester would be back. And she was sure they'd all speculated on why Chester had left her.

Well, let their tongues wag. She had turned down their help. She'd pay hell before she'd take their pity. She'd show them all. Lila Cross Bailey didn't need anyone. Never had.

Tears sprang to her eyes. She furtively wiped them away. The last thing she'd do was let one person in this community see her cry.

Not that there was much left. There were only a half-dozen houses still standing, most of them empty, in what had once been a thriving homestead town a hundred years ago.

Amid the weeds, abandoned houses and what was left of the foundations of homes long gone was Titus and Pearl Cavanaugh's big white three-story house at the far end of the street. Next to it was the smaller house where Titus's mother, Bertie, had lived before she'd become so sick she had to go into Whitehorse to the nursing home.

A couple of blocks behind the community

center and near the creek stood the old abandoned Cherry house, which kids still said was haunted. Lila was eleven when she heard what sounded like a baby crying in the empty old Victorian house. She still got goose bumps when she thought about it.

At the opposite end of town was Geraldine Shaw's clapboard house, a large red barn behind it.

Overlooking the town was the Whitehorse Cemetery, where residents had been buried from the time the original homesteaders settled here. The most recent grave belonged to Abigail Ames, Pearl Cavanaugh's mother. Next to the cemetery was the fairgrounds where community summer events took place.

As Lila looked up, a tumbleweed cartwheeled across Main Street. Like many small towns across eastern Montana, both Old Town and Whitehorse were dying, the young people leaving, the old people heading for the cemetery on the hill.

The young people left for better jobs or to go to school and never return, glad to have escaped the hard life of farming or ranching such austere county.

Lila knew that Faith and McKenna had only come home for the summer because they'd heard that their father had moved out. She'd insisted they take jobs in Whitehorse to keep them out of her hair and make it clear that she didn't need their help.

Not that there was much in Whitehorse to the north. It had a grocery, a newspaper, several banks, a handful of churches and a hardware store and lumberyard. The bowling alley had burned down but the old-timey theater was still open, showing one new movie three days a week.

Like other ranchers from around the county, Lila went into Whitehorse for supplies and to stop by the nursing home to see her mother.

Why Eve had come back was a mystery to most everyone but Lila. Eve moved into her grandmother's house up the road and, from all appearances, seemed to be staying, which frightened Lila more than she wanted to admit.

As she gazed out the window, Lila knew it was just a matter of time before she'd be all alone in that big old rambling house with nothing but memories. And regrets.

"They'll find her," a deep male voice said behind her, making her jump.

She felt the skin on her neck prickle as she recognized the voice and realized he had her trapped in the corner between the long potluck table and the window.

Her back stiffened and she had to fix her expression before she turned around to face Errol Wilson.

"I know you must be worried, but we all know how strong Eve is," Errol said. He was a short, broad man with small dark eyes and a receding hairline of salt-and-pepper hair that stuck out from under his Western hat.

As his eyes locked with hers, Lila felt her skin crawl. She nodded, unable to speak, barely able to breathe. Normally, she made sure she kept her distance from Errol at these community gatherings, never letting him get her alone, even with other people around. But nothing about the past few days had been normal.

"Eve's a survivor," Errol continued, standing next to Lila but not looking at her. So close she knew that no one else in the room could hear him. If anyone looked this way, they would think he was inspecting the dishes that had been set out for the potluck.

"Like her mother," Errol added.

"Ready?" Frank Ross called to Errol. "You're going with Floyd Evans and the sheriff," Frank told Errol, and gave Lila a comforting nod before heading for the door.

Lila turned her back to Errol, but she could still feel him behind her, the scent of his after-shave making her stomach roil.

"Don't worry, Lila," Errol said. "We'll find your daughter and bring her back to you. Wouldn't let anything ever happen to her. Just like I'd hate to see anything happen to you."

She gripped the edge of the table, shaking violently with anger and fear and enough regret that she thought she might drown in it.

Please, God, let Eve be all right. Don't punish her for my mistakes. Give me a chance to make things right with her.

But even as she prayed it, Lila Bailey knew there was no way she could make any of this right with Eve.

CARTER SADDLED up with the search party. After the storm, there would be no passable roads to the south. There were few roads to begin with. A couple of Jeep trails when the weather was good. One road that petered out a couple of miles out near his family's old place.

His father had sold out a while back. Carter's

brother Cade hadn't had any interest in ranching and Deena had flat out refused to live on a ranch. She thought Whitehorse was the end of the earth as it was.

So his father had sold the homestead. Not that Loren Jackson had ever had any interest in ranching. He'd always leased the land. No, Loren had wanted to be a commercial pilot, but for some reason hadn't left Phillips County so he'd ended up crop dusting with his father, Ace Jackson.

That was until he'd up and decided to move to Florida.

Carter had never understood his father. Loren Jackson had always seemed…unfulfilled.

So it felt odd to be here and realize that the old place stood empty just up the road. The Cavanaughs had bought the land, but no one had a use for the house, so it had been boarded up.

Carter rode east to avoid seeing the place, going past Bailey property and the house where he'd heard Eve was staying. One of the search party checked to make sure Eve hadn't returned.

She hadn't. And McKenna had come along to get a change of clothing for Eve to wear when they found her. Then they all rode south, leaving behind farm and ranch land for cactus and sagebrush.

Titus had divided the men into groups, each armed with a two-way radio. Ward Shaw had brought along a saddled extra horse for Eve to ride when they found her. Everyone was optimistic they would find her alive.

Or at least they pretended to be.

The thunderstorm the night before had wiped out any trace of her tracks, but her horse had returned this morning, leaving deep gouges in the wet gumbolike mud that were easy to follow.

The sheriff rode with Errol Wilson and Floyd Evans. The others fanned out, hoping to catch sight of Eve's footprints since she would be on foot.

Although Carter had grown up here and known Errol and Floyd all his life, the three rode in silence with little to say to one another. Both men were older by at least twenty-five years and while Errol and Floyd lived within miles of each other, Carter had never known them to be friends.

In fact, few people in and around Old Town particularly liked Errol Wilson. There was something about the man that put Carter off, as well. Something behind the man's dark eyes that seemed almost predatory. Errol radiated a bitterness for which Carter had never known the source.

As a boy, Carter remembered overhearing some of the men talking about Errol. There was some concern that Errol might be a Peeping Tom. Carter hadn't known what that was at the time. And he'd never heard any more about it. He just figured that men like Errol Wilson generated those kind of stories because they didn't fit in.

Carter gave no more thought to either man as he rode. His mind was on Eve and the argument she'd had with her mother. What had sent Eve riding deep into the Breaks without food or water or proper clothing? Her horse coming back without her was a very bad sign. He was worried what they would find. If they managed to find her at all.

The sun moved across Montana's big sky, drying the mud, heating the air to dragon's breath. No breeze moved the air. Nothing stirred, but an occasional cricket in a clump of brush.

An hour later, Carter reined in as he lost Eve's horse's tracks in a rocky area. "Let's spread out. Holler when you pick up the tracks again," he told the two men.

Errol rode off to the west while Floyd went east, kicking up a bunch of antelope. Carter watched the antelope run across the horizon, disappearing as the land began to drop, funneling forward to the riverbed.

To the west Carter saw one of the other groups from the search party had stopped to clean the mud from their horses' hooves. A hawk soared overheard, picking up a thermal, and nearby a mule deer spooked, rising up from a rocky coulee, all big ears as it took off, kicking up clumps of dried earth. No sign of Eve Bailey.

Carter rode straight south to where the flat, high prairie broke into eroded fingers of land that dropped precariously to the river bottom. He kept to the higher ridges in hopes of seeing Eve's blue T-shirt. The problem was that too much of this land looked exactly the same. That made it extremely easy to get lost. During the storm, Eve could have gotten turned around. If she'd tried to walk out on foot last night she might be anywhere.

At one point, he stopped and realized he could no longer see either Errol or Floyd. He hoped to hell the search party didn't have to find them before the day was over.

He'd just reined in his horse on a narrow ridge, the sides falling dangerously toward the old river bottom when he caught sight of something light blue in the rocks far below him.

REPORTER GLEN WHITAKER couldn't believe his timing. He made it to the Whitehorse Community Center just as Arlene Evans was unloading the pies from the front seat of her pickup.

"Let me help you with those," he said.

Arlene was a gangly woman with an elongated horsy face and laugh that was more donkey's bray. That alone would have put off most people, but there was also a nervous energy that at best made him jittery and at worse made the hair stand up on his arms.

"Violet, say hello to Glen," Arlene ordered.

"Hi, Glen," said a shy and bored voice behind him.

He turned to see Arlene's daughter, Violet.

While better looking than her mother, Violet was still plain to the point of pitiful. Next to her mother, Violet seemed almost catatonic. "Hey," he said.

He'd always suspected that Arlene fed off other people's energy because, like her daughter, Glen found that after a matter of minutes around Arlene he barely had enough energy to escape. And right now escape was exactly what he wanted to do.

"Violet and I can get the pies if you'll open the front door," Arlene said, handing off a pie to her daughter then picking up another before kicking the pickup door shut in one smooth movement.

He had to almost run to get the community center door open before Arlene. They both had to wait for Violet, who moved like sludge.

"Violet, why don't you get Glen a piece of the coconut-custard right away," Arlene said. "He looks like he could use it."

Violet nodded as she wandered off to do as she'd been told. Already trained to obey, she'd make someone the perfect wife, Glen thought. Just not him. At forty, he'd never married. His mother said it was because she'd spoiled him.

"Any news on Eve Bailey?" he asked.

"Apparently not," Arlene said, as she shot a look at the somber group of women waiting in the community center.

All the women looked in his direction, then went back to visiting among themselves or occupying themselves with the needlework in their laps. Glen had never understood it. He was nice enough looking, but for some reason people didn't seem to pay any attention to him.

Feeling like the invisible man, he drew out his notebook and pen as he and Arlene took a seat in a quiet corner and waited for Violet to bring the pie.

"It's a shame," Arlene was saying in a hushed voice so the others couldn't hear. "She has been through so much and now this."

"Eve?" Glen asked, wondering what was keeping Violet.

"Lila," Arlene whispered, glancing in the woman's direction. Lila was cleaning the sink near the back door, stopping periodically to look out, as if she hoped to see her daughter.

Glen wasn't interested in Lila Bailey. No story there.

"Her husband left her, you know. Oh, she tells everyone he moved into Whitehorse to be closer to his job, but we all know the truth."

Arlene took a breath and Glen jumped in, hoping to get some background material, "So what brought Eve Bailey back here?" He watched Arlene shift gears. Apparently she

was just getting warmed up on the Lila and
Chester Bailey story.

"A man," Arlene said flatly. "It's the only
thing that brings a woman her age back to the
ranch. You know she's thirty-two. Just two
years younger than my Violet."

An old maid in Arlene's eyes.

"I heard she became an *interior designer.*"
Arlene lifted a brow as if to say what a waste of
time and education that was. "You can bet some
man broke her heart and she came running home
with her tail tucked between her legs."

Glen wrote on his notepad a new headline:
Jilted, Whitehorse Woman Returns Home
Only To Die Alone In Missouri Breaks.

Violet slid a plate with a large piece of
coconut-custard pie in front of him and sank
into a chair as if the chore had spent all of her
energy.

He glanced at her as he picked up the fork.
"Thanks." She stared back with large, liquid,
colorless eyes, but with just enough expecta-
tion in them to make him nervous. It hit him
then that she would want to get married even
more than her mother wanted her to.
Marriage would be the only way to make her
mother stop trying to hoist her off on men.
Any man.

As he took a bite of pie, he noticed Arlene had stopped talking and was staring toward the front door.

A man in his early thirties who Glen had never seen before stood in the doorway as if looking for someone but not seeing them, turned and left, letting the door close behind him.

"Who was that?" Glen asked, seeing Arlene's obvious interest.

"The fella who's renting the old McAllister place," Arlene whispered. "Bridger Duvall. Sounds like the name of an actor. Or a name he just made up. No one knows anything about him. Or why he rented that old farmhouse, since he hasn't shown any interest in raising a thing. He was downright rude when Violet and I went out there to welcome him to the area."

Glen could well imagine what Arlene's welcome visit was all about—and no doubt the man had, as well, the moment he laid eyes on Violet.

"I wonder," Arlene said slowly. "You know he showed up about the same time Eve returned to town." Her eyes widened. "What if he's the man who broke Eve Bailey's heart?"

And this, Glen thought, was how rumors got started.

SHERIFF CARTER JACKSON felt his breath catch in his throat as he stared down into the ravine. The spot of light blue hadn't moved and, from this angle, he couldn't tell what it was but he had a bad feeling it was Eve Bailey.

He raised his binoculars. The light blue moved. He felt his heart lift like helium. Eve Bailey rose from where she'd been almost hidden in the rocks. He watched her work her way slowly up the slope head down, oblivious to him standing high above her. She climbed the rocks with fluid if exhausted movements.

Carter found himself grinning, overjoyed that she was all right, glad he would be able to take good news back to the Whitehorse Community Center.

Now that he knew she was alive, though, he wanted to wring her neck. What the hell had she been thinking riding out like that yesterday afternoon? Maybe more to the point, what was she doing down in that ravine to begin with?

"I've found her," he said into the two-way radio. "She looks like she's all right. I'm going down to get her out. Bring the horse to the top of the ravine." He gave a reading from his GPS.

Titus Cavanaugh came back over the radio an instant later, sounding equally relieved. "We're not far from you. Glad to hear the good news."

Carter dismounted and, taking his pack with his rescue gear, started to work his way down the rocky slope. His earlier exhilaration at seeing that she was alive was dampened at the thought of what her reaction would be to seeing him. It had been years, but he doubted she would have forgotten the way things had ended between them.

Eve had taken off for college right after high school graduation and he hadn't seen her since. He knew she'd come back for holidays to see her parents and sisters, but she'd made a point of avoiding him. And since he lived in Whitehorse, he'd had no reason to go out of his way to see her.

In fact, the way even the mention of Eve set Deena off, he'd stayed as far away as he could from Old Town—and Eve Bailey.

He was pretty sure Eve hated him. Not that he could blame her. Or maybe she hadn't given him a thought since the day she left.

He wished he could say the same.

As he cut off her ascent up the rocky ravine, he realized he was nervous about seeing her. This was crazy. Hell, it had been years. She'd probably forgotten that night in the front seat of his old Chevy pickup behind her parents' barn.

Just then she looked up and he knew Eve hadn't forgotten—or forgiven him.

Chapter Four

Eve Bailey looked up at the sound of small loose rocks cascading down the side of the ravine. For a moment, she was blinded by the sun and thought she had imagined the dark silhouette of a man working his way down the slope toward her.

But she would have recognized Sheriff Carter Jackson just by the way he moved even if she hadn't seen the glint of the star on his uniform shirt. Her breath caught at the sight of him. Surprise, then that old chest-aching pain kicked in before she could vanquish it with anger.

"Stay there," he called down to her in a deep voice that had once done more than made her poor heart pitter-patter.

She defied her heart to beat even a second faster at the sound of his voice as she stopped to get control of herself. Wasn't that just her luck? Rescued by the one person on earth she'd never wanted to lay eyes on again.

She leaned against one of the large rocks, not wanting to admit how glad she was to see another human being, though. She felt weak with relief. That and hunger and dehydration and exhaustion. She hadn't let herself even consider what she would do once she reached the top of the ravine. She'd have had miles more to walk and, the truth was, she would have never made it, and she knew it.

She wanted to sit down and cry, she was so relieved. But why did her rescuer have to be Carter Jackson? When she'd come home, she'd known she would see him eventually. Whitehorse was too small for her not to run into him.

But the last thing she wanted was for him to see her like this, at her most vulnerable. With Carter, she needed all her defenses, and right now she couldn't have felt more defenseless.

She pushed off the rock, determined not to show any weakness as she started to climb again.

Moving had kept her alive. She was cold and hurt and barely able to keep going. But she'd known that with her clothing still damp, if she'd stopped she would have died. It had been a realistic fear given the temperature earlier this morning and the fact that even with the sun now blazing down, she couldn't seem to get warm.

But there was another reason she'd kept moving. She didn't want to think about what she'd discovered down in the ravine. She shivered at the memory of what she'd had to do to survive. That was her, Eve Bailey, the survivor. Isn't that what she'd heard her whole life? Just like her mother, she thought bitterly.

The climb down the cliff from the plane had been harrowing. She'd fallen more than once, her hands raw, her left ankle killing her.

All she'd known was that she had to find a way down, then back up out of the Breaks no matter how long it took. Given that the crashed plane had apparently never been discovered, she'd figured there was little chance of anyone finding her unless she got off that rock ledge.

She'd been sure it would be days before anyone even realized she was missing, since she lived alone and doubted anyone had seen her ride out yesterday afternoon. Mostly, she worried about her horse. The mare would have gotten out of the storm, but where was she now? Eve loved that horse and couldn't bear it if something had happened to her.

A shadow fell over her. She stopped climbing and looked up, having lost track of time again.

Sheriff Carter Jackson stood on the rocks just above her, his hand outstretched. She didn't look at his face as she reluctantly took his hand and let him pull her up onto a large flat rock, too tired to protest. Her legs gave out and she sat down hard, no longer strong enough to even pretend she was tougher than she was.

Without a word, Carter slipped off his backpack and, opening it, handed her a bottle of water.

"Have you seen my horse? Is she all right?" Eve asked before taking a drink, a catch in her throat.

"Your horse is fine. She returned to the ranch this morning. That's what started the search for you."

"Just like Lassie," she said, near tears, and took a long gulp of the water to hide her relief.

"Just like Lassie," he said with a smile. "Her tracks led us to you."

She kept her focus on the water bottle, furious that all it took to transport her back to their senior year in high school was his smile. She could feel him studying her, his look gentle, concerned. Just as he'd been the night he took her virginity in his old pickup behind her family's barn.

Her hands were shaking, legs trembling, the past twenty-four hours taking their toll. Behind her eyes, she could feel tears welling up. She hurt all over, some of those bruises from years ago and her last encounter with Carter Jackson.

She bit her lip and took another drink as she heard him dig in his pack again. Was he thinking about that night in his pickup? More than likely he was thinking what a fool she'd been to ride so far without water or food, let alone proper clothing.

"Here," he said, and handed her a candy bar.

She took the candy, struggling with the wrapper, her fingers refusing to work properly.

Covering her with his shadow, Carter leaned down to take the candy bar from her, ripped the paper open and handed the bar back to her without a word.

"Thanks." She'd known Carter Jackson all

of her life. They'd gone to the same one-room schoolhouse through elementary school before being bused into Whitehorse for high school.

There'd been something between them from the moment she'd punched him in the nose in grade-school recess to the first time he'd kissed her, something she'd mistaken for love long before she'd given herself to him in his old Chevy pickup.

She brushed a lock of hair back from her face, knowing she must look a mess. "Go on and say it. I know you're dying to. I was an idiot for riding this far out yesterday without any provisions."

"You don't need a lecture," he said quietly. "You've been through enough."

So true, she thought, studying him. Problem was he had no idea what she'd been through. Not years ago when he dumped her for Deena Turner—certainly not last night.

Carter said nothing as he reached into the pack again and this time took out a pair of rolled-up jeans, a flannel shirt and jacket. "McKenna got these for you from your house."

She stared at his handsome face for a moment, the devoured candy bar like a lump in her stomach. Tears burned her eyes. She'd been so scared, so afraid she'd never get back to the ranch, never see the people she cared about again that she hadn't realized how much she'd scared her family and neighbors. Of course, they would be worried sick about her.

If it had been anyone but Carter who'd found her, she would have wept with joy at being rescued. But she couldn't break down, not with Carter—and trying not to cry had left her raw with emotion.

She took the dry clothing, desperately needing to get moving before she couldn't anymore. The sugar from the candy bar was trying to jump-start her dog-tired body, but knowing that she no longer had to push herself to get home again all she wanted to do was curl up on a warm rock and sleep for a week.

"The…underwear is in the jacket pocket," Carter said, sounding almost shy as he turned his back to let her change.

She couldn't help but remember the last time he'd handed her her clothes. She'd been naked then, though, and even more vulnerable than she was now.

The warm, dry clothing felt wonderful, although it took her a while to get her wet clothes off, her movements awkward and slow. She realized how close she'd been to hypothermia, how close she'd been to dying if she'd stopped even to rest too long earlier.

As she pulled on the jacket, she hugged herself, feeling warmer for the first time in what seemed like days.

With a start she remembered what she'd left in the pocket of her wet jeans. Quickly she checked to make sure Carter's back was still turned before she reached into the front pocket of her dirty torn jeans and, with shaking fingers, transferred the rhinestone pin she'd found in the plane to her clean jeans pocket before saying, "All done."

He turned to look at her. "Better?"

She nodded, fearing he could see the guilt written all over her face. But maybe he didn't know her as well as she knew him. Maybe he never had.

He handed her another bottle of water, picking up the empty one from where she'd placed it on a rock and putting it back into his pack.

She opened the cap and took a long drink, trying to get control of her emotions. She could feel the weight of her old feelings for him heavy in her stomach. Just as she could feel the sharp edges of the rhinestones poking her upper thigh, prodding her conscience.

She dug for anger to steady herself, recalling the morning she reached school to find out that after being with her, Carter had been with Deena Turner. Deena had told everyone at school and announced that they were going steady. Nothing hurt like high school, she thought, but even the memory couldn't provide enough anger to balance out her guilt.

She had to tell Carter about the plane.

Even if it meant betraying her own family.

CARTER STUDIED EVE, worried. He knew her too well, he realized, even after all these years. One of the things he'd always liked about her was her directness. She said what was on her mind.

But he could see that she was fighting more than exhaustion, as if trying too hard not to let him know just how bad last night had been. The fact that she hadn't said anything made him fear she was in more trouble than being caught without her horse in a storm in the Breaks.

"I *am* curious how you lost your horse, though," he said as he stuffed the dirty clothing she'd rolled up into his pack. "You get bucked off?"

Her head jerked up, her dark eyes hot with indignation. "You know darned well I haven't been thrown from a horse since I was—"

"Nine," he said. "I remember." He remembered a lot of things about her, including her stubborn pride—and the moonlight on her face their last night together.

Her eyes narrowed as if she, too, remembered only too well things she would prefer to forget.

"McKenna told me that you and your mom had words just before you rode out yesterday," he said.

"McKenna," Eve said like a curse. "Did she also fill you in on what it was about?"

He shook his head. "Apparently she didn't hear that part."

Eve gave him a wan smile. Nothing more.

"How'd you come to be way down there? It's not like you to end up without your horse in the bottom of a ravine."

"You don't know what I'm like anymore," she snapped, looking back down the steep rocky slope.

"Okay, if you don't want to tell me…" he said as he slung the pack over his shoulder.

"I found something." She said it grudgingly.

He looked down at her, hearing something in her voice that instantly set his heart racing. She was biting down on her lower lip, looking scared. "What?"

"Hey down there!" Errol Wilson called from the top of the gulch. "Everything all right?" A shower of small rocks cascaded down just feet from them.

"She's fine," Carter called back, irritated at the interruption. "Make sure everyone stays back. The ground is unstable and breaking off up there."

"Sure." Errol sounded disappointed, either that the rescue adventure was over already or that Carter had shooed him away.

When Errol stepped away, disappearing from the edge, Carter turned again to Eve. He'd seen Eve Bailey vulnerable only once before. He shoved aside the memory of her in his arms, her bare skin pressed to his, the windows steaming up on his old Chevy pickup....

"You *found* something?" he repeated.

She rubbed her ankle, wincing as if it hurt. "I found a body."

He felt his stomach clench even as he told himself she had to be mistaken. He'd had his share of calls from residents who'd uncovered bones and erroneously thought they'd found human remains.

Eve shook her head as if she still couldn't believe it herself. She drained the contents of the second water bottle before she spoke. "It was in a plane that had crashed in the ravine."

"An airplane?" he echoed as he looked down into the deep gorge and saw nothing. If there'd been a plane crash out here, he'd have heard about it.

"It was a small one, a four-seater," she said, her voice sounding hollow. "It's been there for a long time."

"Where?"

She glanced to the west. "Back that way. I'm not sure how far. I lost track trying to find a way out of there. But I'll know the ravine when I see it."

He hoped so, but the ravines all looked alike and in the state she was in… "The pilot was still in the plane?" he asked, thinking about the body she'd said she found.

"Not the pilot," she said without looking at him. "One of the passengers." She raised her eyes, locking with his for just an instant before she looked away again.

She'd found a crashed airplane in a ravine with the body of one of the passengers still in it and she hadn't said anything about it until now? The old Eve Bailey would have blurted it out the moment she saw him.

But then he and the old Eve Bailey had been friends. Lovers. The old Eve Bailey would have trusted him.

Maybe she was right. Maybe he didn't know her anymore. But he knew that wasn't the case. Because just looking into her face, he'd seen that she hadn't wanted to tell him about the plane.

The realization shocked him. Why would she keep something like that to herself?

He took a breath and let it out slowly. "You say the plane looked as if it had been there for a while?"

"Thirty-two years."

He sat down on a rock across from her so they were eye to eye. "What makes you think it's been there for thirty-two years?"

She continued rubbing her ankle for a moment before looking up at him. "There was a logbook in the cockpit. The last entry was February seven, 1975."

Carter couldn't believe this. His grandfather and father, both crop dusters, lived and breathed airplanes. They would have known about a missing plane. There would have been a search for the plane and, when found, the body removed even if it was impossible to get the plane out.

Unless the plane had never been reported missing.

He looked at Eve and felt a jolt. There was more.

"The passenger in the plane," she said, her voice almost a whisper. Her gaze met his. "He has a knife sticking out of his chest. At least I think it was a man."

From above them came the sound of more voices, the whinny of horses and more small rocks showering down.

Carter rose, shaken. "I'm going to ask you not to say anything about this to anyone," he said to her.

She looked up at him and nodded slowly.

"Do you think you can tell me where you found the plane?" he asked.

She shook her head. "It's hidden. If not for the storm, I wouldn't have seen anything down there. I'll have to take you to it."

"No, you need to go back with the search party so you can get medical treatment, food, rest."

"I'm fine." She rose to her feet with obvious difficulty. "I assume you brought me a horse?"

"Titus has one up on top for you, but Eve—"

"I told you, I'm fine." She glanced toward the canyon far below them, then at him as if she could read his mind. "Don't worry, I can find the plane again. Maybe you've forgotten, but I grew up here. I know this country."

Unlike Deena, the woman he'd dumped her for. The woman he'd stupidly married, divorced and was still trying to get out of his life. Deena didn't know one end of a horse from the other and she could get lost in the city park. Deena would never have survived five minutes out here last night.

"Eve—"

"I really need to get moving."

He nodded, not even sure what he'd planned to say. Whatever it was, this wasn't the time or the place to talk about the past. "I'll be right behind you."

They climbed out of the ravine, using the exposed rocks like steps. He could see that Eve was dead on her feet. She needed sleep, a hot shower, real food.

But she seemed to draw on some inner strength that the dry clothing and candy bar and water had little to do with. Eve was a strong woman. Isn't that what he'd told himself so many years ago, that Eve Bailey was strong. She'd get over any pain he'd caused her.

He'd lied to himself because he couldn't face the fact that he'd hurt Eve.

IT TOOK THE LAST of her resources to get to the top of the ravine, but Eve was bound and determined. She reached the top to cheers of the search party, making her feel even more foolish, as she apologized for wasting their time, although they all insisted it had been no trouble.

"So what happened?" Errol Wilson asked.

Whenever Eve saw Errol, she thought of Halloween night when she was five. Her father had taken her to a party at the community center. Her mother had stayed home, complaining of a headache.

In Eve's excitement to tell her mother about the party, she'd been the first out of the truck and racing up the steps to the house when she thought she saw Errol Wilson hiding in the dark at the edge of the porch.

Startled, Eve had let out a bloodcurdling scream and tripped and fell, skinning her knees. Her father had come running, but when Eve looked toward the end of the porch, there wasn't anyone there.

She'd tried to tell her parents that she'd seen a scary man, but they hadn't believed her, saying she'd just imagined it.

All Eve knew was that every time she saw Errol Wilson after that he seemed to have a smug look on his face, as if the two of them shared a secret. The smugness had only intensified after he'd seen her yesterday when he was coming out of her mother's back door.

"Eve was thrown from her horse and ended up at the bottom of a ravine," Carter said before Eve could answer.

She shot him a withering look. "I'd prefer that story not get back to my sisters, if you don't mind. I will never live it down."

Everyone laughed. Except Errol.

"Eve, you should know how hard it is to keep a secret in Whitehorse," he said.

"Eve and I are going to take it slow on the way back," Carter said, and looked over at Eve as if wondering what Errol had meant by that. "I'd appreciate it if the rest of you would go back and let everyone know that Eve is fine."

"I know your mother will be relieved," Errol said. "She worries about you. I'm glad I can relieve her mind."

Eve couldn't suppress a shudder as she saw him look back at her as he rode off with the others.

Apparently she and Errol Wilson now shared another secret. One he worried she would tell?

CARTER FROWNED as he saw Eve's reaction to Errol. What had that odd exchange been about, he wondered.

As Eve reached for the reins of the horse Titus had brought her, Carter saw her wince with pain.

"Here," he said, drawing her attention away from Errol. "Let me put something on your hands."

"I'm fine," she snapped.

"You're not fine," he said, hooking her elbow and pulling her over to a rock. "Sit down. You're limping. You need that ankle wrapped. I can tell from here that it's swollen. You also need something on your hands."

Evidently she didn't want him to touch her. He couldn't blame her. In fact, he was still surprised she hadn't laid into him, telling him off good. He knew she wanted to, so why was she holding back? Did she think he didn't know he'd hurt her?

Finding the plane and the dead man inside must have shaken her up more than he could imagine. Or was something else bothering her, he wondered, as he looked to where Errol Wilson and the rest of the search party had ridden off.

Eve closed her eyes and leaned back as if soaking up the sun—and ignoring him as he gently wrapped her ankle.

Her hands were bruised and scraped raw. They had to be killing her. "This is going to burn," he said as he turned up her palms and applied the spray.

She didn't make a sound, her eyes closed tight. If it hadn't been for the one lone tear that escaped her lashes, he would have believed it didn't faze her.

"I'm sorry," he said quietly. "I didn't mean to hurt you."

Her eyes blinked open. He looked into that moist deep darkness and saw the pain and anger. "You didn't hurt me." She pulled back her hands. "Can we please get this over with?"

He nodded and put everything back into his pack. He didn't kid himself. He'd pay hell before ever getting back in Eve's good graces. It would be a waste of time to even try. She'd never forgive him and he couldn't blame her.

But as he swung up onto his horse, knowing better than to offer Eve any help getting on hers, he vowed to move heaven and earth, if that's what it took, for the chance.

LIGHT-HEADED and beyond exhaustion, Eve found she also ached all over as she swung up into the saddle.

She'd seen Carter's worried look and suspected she looked like a woman who'd fallen down a mountainside. She had.

But none of that was as painful as having to sit there while Carter Jackson saw to her injuries. It was the gentle way he touched her, reminding her of their lovemaking the one and only time they'd been together. It was his concerned expression. For an awful moment, he sounded as if he was about to apologize for breaking her heart.

Eve Bailey could take a lot, but she couldn't take that.

They rode west, working their way along the top of the ridges, the land dropping precariously to the old river bottom. She could feel the piece of costume jewelry in her pocket biting into her flesh as if mocking her for feeling so righteous when it came to Carter.

She argued that the way he'd betrayed her—and her keeping the pin in her pocket from him—weren't the same thing at all.

The lie caught in her throat like dust. But to admit she'd recognized the pin and knew who it belonged to would be to consider that her family had something to do with that plane and—worse—the dead man inside it. It was easier to lie and pray it was a coincidence that the plane had gone down just miles from the Bailey ranch.

Eve still felt chilled in the dry clothing, although the day was warm as the sun dipped toward the western horizon. Hours had passed without her even noticing it. As she rode, she watched for the ravine where she'd found the plane.

In the distance, she recognized an outcropping of rocks and knew they weren't far now. She glanced over at Carter.

How easy it would have been to keep riding, to pretend she'd gotten turned around, to leave the plane and its secrets buried where she'd found it.

"We getting close?" he asked, as if he'd caught her indecision.

She'd been wrong about him not knowing her anymore. He knew she couldn't pretend to have lost the location of the plane. Any more than she could pretend he hadn't broken her heart.

CARTER REINED in his horse next to Eve's. Below them was another steep ravine much like the others they'd passed.

He glanced over at Eve. What had her running scared? Eve wasn't squeamish when it came to dead animals. True, seeing a body would have upset her, but it wouldn't have her scared. So what was going on with her?

"Is it down there?" he asked. All he could see was a thick stand of junipers growing out of a rock ledge at least halfway down the steep ravine.

She nodded, looking ill.

"You went down there?" He couldn't see anything that would have tempted him into sliding down that slope.

"I heard a moan. I thought there was someone down there." Her voice broke. "It was just the wind blowing over the metal of the plane."

"The plane is in the junipers?" He couldn't help sounding skeptical.

She looked down into the ravine. "That's why it's never been found I would imagine."

He couldn't believe the chance she'd taken going down there. But Eve wouldn't have thought about her own safety if she thought there was someone down there injured.

He had to see the plane and body for himself

and that meant going down there. He'd have to be quick. He needed to get her back to her house. He felt badly about putting her through this. But he feared if he had waited until tomorrow, Eve might have changed her mind about showing him where the plane was. Although he couldn't imagine why.

"Will you be all right up here?" he asked, worried about her.

She slid off her horse, practically collapsing as her boot soles hit the ground. "Leave me some water and your hat. I lost mine. I'll just rest while you're gone."

He dismounted and, pulling down his pack, reached inside for his rain jacket. Rolling it up, he handed it to her. "Put your head on this," he said, clearing a spot for her on the soft sun-dried earth.

She did as he said without even an argument. He knew she was simply too exhausted to put up a fight today. Eve hadn't changed. And that's what made this so painful. He'd been such a fool to throw her over for a woman like Deena.

Her eyes opened and narrowed as if she knew what he was thinking. "You still here?"

"I'll be right back," he said.

She nodded and closed her eyes again.

Leaving her water and the rest of the candy bars he'd brought, he stepped to the edge of the ravine. He could see faint tracks where she'd slid down and where the rain had eroded the earth even more during the storm last night.

He glanced back at her, amazed she wasn't worse off given what she had to have been through. A thought struck him. It had stormed all night. How had she…

Her lashes fluttered as she opened them again just enough to squint at him.

And he knew how she'd managed to survive the night in the storm. She'd spent it in the plane with a corpse.

Chapter Five

By early afternoon, word had spread throughout the county that Eve Bailey had been found safe and sound.

It had been all Lila could do not to break down, her relief had been so great. She'd insisted on staying at the center and cleaning up before the sewing group, not wanting to be alone. Also not ready to face her daughter.

Most of the food had been eaten, but she helped put the rest in the refrigerator for when the sheriff and Eve returned. If they didn't stop by the community center she would take some over to Eve later.

Lila knew her daughter. She hated having a fuss made over her, especially concerning something like this where the whole town was involved.

Eve would send her thanks and go straight

home. She'd always been a willful girl, stubborn to the core. Chester used to say she was just like Lila.

The men from the search party had all gone back to their work and McKenna and Faith had gone on into Whitehorse to their summer jobs.

This morning there'd been a sense of purpose, everyone busy doing what they could to help. But now things had returned to normal. Well, as normal as this part of Montana could be, Lila thought.

Now the Whitehorse Sewing Circle could get back to its latest project, making a quilt for Maddie Cavanaugh's upcoming marriage. A community tradition, every newlywed and every newborn had a quilt made by the women who sat around the center quilting by hand.

There were the usual members in attendance today: Wanda Wilson—Errol's wife, Alice White, Ella Cavanaugh, Geraldine Shaw, Arlene Evans and Lila. Carly Matthews was visiting her sister in Great Falls.

Pearl Cavanaugh was the only one of the longstanding quilters missing. She had been admitted last night with walking pneumonia. She'd sent word, though, that she was feeling better. Lila worried that her visit yesterday evening with Pearl had caused her to get sicker. Lila felt sick herself.

There wasn't much talk as the women pulled their chairs up to the quilting frame and busied themselves threading their needles.

Lila went right to work, hating that her fingers were trembling as she made her first stitch. Relief had left her weak and worn-out, worry had made her queasy.

She knew the other women must wonder why she didn't go home to wait for her daughter. Wasn't that what a mother would do after having such a scare? But Lila Bailey had had many scares in her life. A life of tedious day-to-day routine with moments of sheer panic.

That was how it was when your life was built on lies.

Her fingers shook as she made neat, careful stitches in the colorful cloth. If only she could stitch her life back together as easily.

"You're especially quiet today," Arlene commented.

Lila's head shot up only to find that Arlene

wasn't talking to her. Instead, Arlene was staring at Geraldine Shaw.

"Geraldine?" Arlene said as she inspected the size of the stitches Alice was putting into the quilt. "Are you all right?"

Geraldine looked up and blinked as if she'd been miles away. She was a sturdy middle-aged woman, born of Scandinavian stock, thick of body with watery blue eyes and a plain round face. Her graying hair was cut as if a bowl had been placed on her head, the ends chopped just above her slack jaw.

"I'm fine," Geraldine said, forcing her downturned mouth into a smile before her face went slack again.

For an instant, Lila met the woman's gaze across the quilting frame. She thought she saw something in Geraldine's eyes. Something she recognized. Fear.

"How are the wedding plans coming along?" Lila asked, turning back to her quilting.

"Fine," Arlene said and seemed a little too intent on her quilting.

"Your son getting cold feet?" Ella asked Arlene.

"I just think they're too young to be getting married, if you must know," Arlene said.

Lila noticed that no one disagreed. Maddie,

who had just turned eighteen, had given up a scholarship to the university in Missoula to marry Bo. And as far as Lila could tell, Bo, who still lived at home at twenty, didn't have any means of employment.

"I got married young," Alice said. "It all worked out just fine." Alice was nearly ninety and was married almost sixty years when her husband passed away.

"I heard Maddie's been helping over at your place, Geraldine," Arlene said with an edge to her voice that made Lila look up.

Geraldine Shaw let out a cry as she stabbed her finger with her needle. She dropped the needle to suck the blood from her finger, her eyes downcast and bright with tears.

"Did you stick yourself, Geraldine?" Arlene asked.

"It's nothing," Geraldine replied, and picked up her needle again, all her attention on her work.

"I think it's wonderful that Maddie helps you out around the place now that Ollie is gone," Ella said.

Geraldine only nodded and kept quilting.

Arlene looked as if she had something more to say but fortunately Alice jumped in and told a story about her granddaughter.

Lila hated the undercurrents she felt at the

table and wished sometimes that she could just gag Arlene Evans to shut her up.

"Did you see that man who's renting the old McAllister place?" Arlene asked, moving on to greener pastures. "Bridger Duvall. That can't really be his name. He stopped in earlier as if looking for someone." She raised her eyes, taking in each woman at the table, stopping on Lila.

"I heard he's writing a book about White-horse," Alice said. "Including Old Town."

"Really?" Arlene sounded skeptical. "I don't know why, but I got the impression he was looking for Eve."

Lila stared at Arlene, too dumbstruck for a moment to speak. "You're obviously mistaken," she said, jamming her needle through the cloth. "He was probably just wondering what was going on with all the vehicles parked outside."

Arlene lifted a brow. "All he had to do was ask."

"Well, if he was looking for Eve he would have been with the search party, now wouldn't he," Lila said logically.

Logic always stumped Arlene, who thrived on gossip. Unfortunately, she often got it wrong. Why would the man be writing a book on Whitehorse? Or looking for Eve?

CARTER TOOK THE ROPE from his pack and tied it to the saddle. His brother, Cade, had bought some land north of Whitehorse with a rodeo grounds on it. When Carter wasn't acting as sheriff, he calf roped at the arena. He liked being on the back of the horse the way his father apparently liked being in a plane high in the air.

"I should warn you," Eve said without opening her eyes. "That first step into the ravine is a lulu."

Well, he couldn't take the time to find a better way down. He tightened his gloved hands around the rope, pulling on it until he felt resistance from the horse and stepped off the edge of the ravine.

Just as he'd known it would, the top level of the steep incline began to avalanche downward with him.

The horse, trained for roping cattle, kept the line taut as he rappelled down the steep slope. He tried to imagine Eve doing this without a rope. Without a net. The woman was fearless. Crazy, too.

When he reached the rock ledge, he tied off the rope, then worked his way cautiously along the junipers, imagining Eve doing the same. The woman really was something else, he thought as he peered back over the rim of the ledge. Eve had always been afraid of heights, but that hadn't stopped her when she thought there was someone in the junipers who needed her help.

He was beginning to suspect that Eve had been mistaken about this being the ravine when he caught the glint of sun off metal. It shocked him how well hidden the plane was. It was conceivable that the craft wouldn't have been found even if it had been reported missing. Not that he believed it had, given what Eve said was inside the cockpit.

One wing had plowed into the side of the ravine, completely burying it. The other was lost in the juniper branches and, after all these years, woven into the new growth to make the plane impossible to see from above.

It still amazed him that Eve had seen it.

As he moved closer, he saw that she was right. The plane had been there for a long while.

"It's a Navion," he said out loud in surprise as he moved closer. A friend of his father's had one down in Florida. Only about two thousand were built, most back in the 1940s, and none had been built since. They were now popular with collectors because they had held up well, being one of the first metal private planes from that era.

"Wow, it's in fantastic shape given where it ended up." He realized he was talking to himself, something he'd been doing a lot of lately.

As he moved to the cockpit, he held his breath. It was just as Eve had described it. The plane had been well preserved. The sliding canopy—the only way into the cockpit—had remained intact, the windows unbroken but dirty. A strip of torn red cloth was caught in the edge of the canopy. The fabric hung down the side, still wet from the storm.

He could see where Eve had wiped away some of the grime to look inside. He bent closer.

The pilot seat and front passenger seats were empty, but stained as if the occupants might have been injured in the crash. The corpse was strapped in the rear seat, the body mummified over the years. The skin was dried and brown, shrunk to the skeleton, the eye sockets hollow. The shirt was threadbare, even the bloodstain from the wound faded, the jeans in surprisingly good shape, the boots looking like new.

Carter had heard of bodies mummifying under certain conditions but this was the first he'd seen. Eve had said the last entry in the logbook was February. The body would have frozen, then thawed slowly as the months warmed and not decomposed like it would have if the plane had gone down in the summer.

Stuck between two ribs, just as Eve had said, was a hunting knife, the handle grayed with age.

"Damn," Carter said under his breath.

He could see where Eve had climbed into the cockpit. He swore again, imagining her spending the night in there, the storm raging around her, a mummified body in the seat behind her.

He stared at the plane, then at the only way out of here, down a minefield of boulders. Had anyone from the plane gotten out alive?

Carter felt the air around him change. A storm was blowing in again. He had to see to Eve. The last thing he wanted was for her to get caught in another storm, and storms came up so fast out here.

He didn't want to leave the crime scene, but he had no choice. After all, the plane had apparently been here for thirty-two years. What was another day?

As soon as he could get to a landline, he would call the crime lab in Missoula. His cell wouldn't work out here. He could barely get service in Whitehorse.

It was all he could do not to slide back the plane's canopy and have a look around in the cockpit. But the crime scene had been disturbed enough.

He tried to imagine himself spending the night in the close quarters of the cockpit with the mummified murdered man. Eve was more resilient than he'd ever imagined. But then the survival instinct was a strong one. Just like the killer instinct.

Carter worked his way along the junipers, careful with his footing, too aware of the long drop to the bottom of the canyon below him.

He untied the rope from the juniper branch, gave it a tug, then another before he felt tension on the line as the horse responded. Slowly, he began to climb out of the deep ravine. He could smell the promise of rain in the air. June in Montana was like spring most other places. Squalls would blow through, biting cold rain and sleet drenching everything, taking the heat and sun with them.

By the time he reached flat land at the top

of the ravine, he was winded, his palms burning from the rope even through his gloves. Just as he suspected, thunderheads loomed on the horizon. A breeze had come up and in the distance he could see a dust devil whirling through the sagebrush.

Eve was sitting up, watching him as he unhooked the rope from his saddle. The breeze whipped her long dark hair around her face. She squinted at him as if trying to gauge his reaction to what he'd found in the plane. "Well?"

"The plane is right where you said it was."

She nodded. "Any idea who he is?"

"None."

"What happens now?" she asked.

"I get the techs from the crime lab to come down and retrieve the body and any evidence. Let's get you back to your house before this storm hits," he said as he coiled up the rope, worried about her.

She still had a scared look as she glanced toward home and slowly rose from the ground, clearly hesitant. "You think we'll ever know who he is?"

The murdered man in the plane? "Forensics can do amazing things nowadays. I wouldn't be surprised if they were able to get some

DNA on him." He didn't add, though, that it would be worthless unless they had a suspect's DNA to compare it to. "If anyone else in the plane got out alive…"

Eve looked over at him, as if she'd already considered that. If anyone had gotten out alive, they would have walked to the closest place—her family's ranch.

EVE FELT HIS FOCUS ON HER as she swung up into the saddle. Carter made her uncomfortable. Because she felt guilty? Or because just a look from him still made her a little weak in the knees? It infuriated her that she could feel anything for him.

"I need you not to mention the plane to anyone until I can get the crime lab in there," he said.

She nodded.

"Eve, about this fight you had with your mother yesterday…"

She blinked, surprised by his sudden change of subject. For a moment, she'd been so intent on the man that she'd forgotten Carter was also the sheriff. "What does that have to do with anything?"

"I don't know. I'm asking you."

She shook her head. "If you're asking if I

knew about the plane, I didn't. I told you. I wouldn't even have seen it if the storm hadn't kicked up."

He nodded and glanced toward the horizon. She could see the clouds building up again. They'd be lucky to get back to her place before it hit. She spurred her horse, riding past him and toward home.

"Do you remember what you might have touched in the plane?" he asked, catching her and riding along beside her.

"No, I…" Her voice trailed off. It had been a nightmare climbing into the plane and closing the canopy to keep out the cold and sleet. She'd huddled in the seat, the body directly behind her. She could feel his sightless eye sockets fixed on her. Every sound convinced her the body had come alive and was intent on vengeance, starting with her.

Worse than those nightmares was the fear that it hadn't been just her bad luck that she'd stumbled across the plane.

"I don't remember what I might have touched," she said finally. "I was cold and scared. I saw the logbook on the floor and picked it up. I think that's all." The pin in her pocket bit into her flesh. *Liar.*

"OKAY." Carter couldn't shake the feeling that Eve was keeping something from him. Yet he had no choice but to take her word for it. At least for now.

The lab would find her fingerprints. Soon enough he'd know. He stole a glance at her as they rode toward Old Town. She was worrying her lower lip with her teeth, frowning. He wondered what she was worried about. Not that she would ever tell him.

Cursing himself, he rode in silence. Even if he'd known what to say to her, he doubted she'd want to hear it. And what was there to say? He'd been a damn fool. He'd made the mistake of his life sleeping with Deena, let alone marrying her.

Hell, everyone already knew that—the divorce had made that obvious. And everyone had probably heard about the stunts Deena had pulled, including sleeping with his best friend.

He'd blown any chance he ever had with Eve. Why couldn't he accept that?

She had him worried, though. Something was troubling her. Maybe, like him, she feared about the repercussions news of the plane—and the murdered man inside—were going to have on Old Town and Whitehorse.

Word would get out once the crime lab showed up with its vans and helicopter. The news would travel like a grass fire. There was no getting around it.

He just hoped to hell that none of the occupants of that plane were tied to the town. Unfortunately, his family had lived just this side of Old Town thirty-two years ago and he doubted it would slip anyone's mind that both his father and grandfather had been pilots.

In fact, there'd been a grass airstrip on the Jackson ranch not that far from where the Navion had gone down.

Chapter Six

Eve couldn't wait for Carter to leave. He'd come into her grandmother's house to use the phone, stepping around the ladder and cans of paint. "So you're fixing up the place," he'd said as he glanced at the variety of paint colors she'd tried on the living room wall so far. His eyes had widened a little.

He hadn't commented on her bright color choices.

Just as well, since she was in no mood for his opinion.

He'd made a couple of calls. She'd done her best not to listen. He'd called the crime lab in Missoula, then his office to let them know he wouldn't be back the rest of the day. While he'd told whomever he spoke to at the crime lab about the plane, he hadn't mentioned it to whoever he'd talked to at his office.

All she'd wanted was for him to leave so she could finally have a hot shower and forget for a while about the plane—and the rhinestone pin and murdered man. Forget about Carter.

She hugged herself against the wind that whipped her hair around her face as she walked him out to the porch. Any minute it would start raining again.

He didn't seem to want to leave her. "You should have Doc take a look at that ankle. And you won't forget about not mentioning the plane to anyone. At least until you hear from me. You *will* hear from me."

It sounded like a promise. Or, in her state of mind, a threat.

"Fine," she said, and went inside. When she peeked out just before she closed the door, he was still standing on her porch. She waited until she heard him ride off before she headed upstairs.

Once in her bathroom, she turned on the shower, stripped down and stepped under the steaming water. But not even the hot shower could chase away the chill that had settled in her bones. She ached all over and was scraped and bruised in places she hadn't even realized.

Exhaustion dragged at her, but she forced herself to shampoo her hair, standing under the spray to let the water run over her long dark hair.

As she shut off the shower and stepped out, she caught her reflection in the mirror across the large bathroom. The glass had steamed up, but she could still see the dark-haired child she'd been. Her sisters and parents were fair, blond and blue eyed. She, on the other hand, had hair the color of walnut and dark brown eyes. She was the duckling in a family of swans.

She had hated being different as a child.

As an adult, her dissimilarity just made her suspicious.

CARTER RODE his horse back to the truck to get what he'd need to spend the night in the Breaks. Growing up in this isolated country he'd learned a long time ago to carry survival gear in any kind of weather and enough food and water to last for at least a few days.

There was always the likelihood of going off the road and being stranded for days until someone came along or the county got the road open. Each year someone would go off the road or get stuck and think they could walk out for help instead of staying with the vehicle. A fatal decision more times than not. Out here, you did what you had to survive. Just like Eve had done.

He was tying his sleeping bag onto his horse when Lila Bailey came out of the community center. From her dour expression, he thought she hadn't heard the news that Eve had been found.

"Eve's fine. She's at her house. Her grandmother's house," he added, curious if she was fixing the place up because she planned to stay. "She's exhausted. I doubt she'll be coming down to the community center."

Lila nodded as if that was no surprise to her and he noticed then that she carried two foil-wrapped bundles in her hands. "You're going back out?"

"I saw some mountain lion tracks. Just want to check it out," he said.

Her face was expressionless, but still he suspected she knew he was lying. "You'll want to take some food with you." She handed him one of the wrapped items. It felt heavy. "I saw you loading your supplies on your horse so I assumed you weren't done for the day."

"Thanks."

Without another word, she walked to her pickup parked in front of the center, her back straight as a steel rod. As she drove away, he noticed there were still a couple of rigs left, including Glen Whitaker's, the reporter from the Whitehorse local newspaper.

Carter hurried, not in the mood for an interview. Glen would be beating down his door soon enough for the story once he heard about the plane—and the body inside.

As the sheriff swung up into the saddle, wind whipped the tall grass, keeling it over, and the first drops of rain began to fall. He hunkered down in his slicker, noticing that the women still inside the community center were watching him from the window as he rode away.

He wondered if any of them knew about the plane. Or all of them. They were old enough. And as close-knit as this community was he could see the whole town keeping the plane a secret—if they had good reason. He couldn't imagine what that reason would be, though. Not when it involved murder.

But maybe it depended on who was dead in that plane.

If the survivors had managed to walk away from the plane crash, they would have needed help. And help was only a few miles north at one of the ranches—the closest being the

Baileys' ranch. Unless they had gone more to the northwest, then it would have been his family's.

Carter realized it might all depend on what the plane was doing flying this way in the first place. There was more than a remote possibility the pilot had been planning to land on Carter's family's airstrip. It was far enough from the ranch house and Whitehorse. Remote, but it had been February if Eve was right about the logbook entry being the last one.

More than likely the pilot had just gotten lost in the storm and his destination was Glasgow.

At least that's what Carter wanted to believe. Just as he wanted the passengers and pilot to be total strangers. Much better to believe that they couldn't have survived after the crash, the blizzard, the climb out of that ravine.

That way no one in Old Town would have been involved. That people he'd known his whole life wouldn't have been keeping the secret about the plane. Or the murder. And that this had nothing to do with his family. Or Eve's.

EVE HAD JUST GOTTEN dressed when she heard her mother's pickup coming along the lane. From her upstairs window, she watched Lila pull into the yard and cut the engine. Eve waited. She couldn't see her mother's face through the rain-streaked windshield of the pickup, but she could sense her indecision.

It was late afternoon. The worst of the storm had blown through. Eve could see a sliver of clear sky peeking through the clouds to the west, the sun long gone. A light rain still fell, dimpling the puddles left in her yard, leaving a chill in the air.

The pickup door finally opened. Her mother stepped out, avoiding the puddles as she ran through the drizzle toward the house.

Eve turned from the window, and with dread, headed down the stairs. She wasn't up to continuing their argument. And what was there to say, anyway? Her mother was cheating on her father. And with Errol Wilson, if that wasn't bad enough.

When Eve opened the door, she found her mother standing on the porch looking off toward the Breaks.

The doorbell hadn't rung. Nor had her mother knocked. In fact, Eve had the impression that Lila Bailey might have left had Eve not opened the door when she had.

Lila turned toward her, appearing startled out of her thoughts and looking confused, as if she'd forgotten why she'd stopped by. She held something foil wrapped. Food, no doubt. Her mother's idea of love was cooking something for her family. Eve suspected it was avoidance.

"I wanted to make sure you were all right," her mother said. "I can't stay. I just brought you some of Arlene's casserole that you like." She held it out to Eve, but Eve didn't take it.

"Mother, please, come in," Eve said, stepping back. "I was going to come see you anyway."

Lila didn't look happy about either prospect. She had to know that their discussion from yesterday wasn't finished. Her mother was the kind of woman who stuck her head in the sand, hoping that when she came up for air the problem would be gone and forgotten.

It amazed Eve that her mother seemed to be taking the same attitude with her husband, pretending that Chester had moved out just to be closer to his job. The same attitude she'd taken when Eve returned wanting answers.

Wind whirled cold, damp air through the open doorway. "You can take a few minutes, I'm sure," she said. "I need to show you something."

Her mother hesitated, surveying the paint cans and ladder. Clearly she hadn't expected the conversation to take this turn and was curious about what Eve wanted to show her.

"I see you're changing the place," she said, sounding disapproving as she gingerly stepped around the paint cloths on the hardwood floor and Eve closed the door behind her.

"I really need to get back to the center. Pearl is in the hospital and if we're going to get this quilt done before Maddie and Bo get married…" Lila stopped just inside the living room.

Yes, Eve thought. Her mother always had somewhere she had to be when Eve wanted answers.

"So which color do you like best?" Eve asked, as if that was her only reason for wanting her mother to come in.

Lila glanced at the bright paint smears on the wall and seemed to be trying to think of something nice to say. "They're all fine."

Eve chuckled. The walls at the farmhouse where Eve was raised had had the original wallpaper—until her father moved out. Eve noticed Lila had painted over them. Everything was now white.

Had her mother done that as a fresh start? Or had she been dying to paint over the wallpaper for years? Eve had no idea. Her mother kept her feelings, as well as her own counsel, to herself.

"Pick the one you like. You're the one who's going to be staying here for a while. I really need to get back." Lila started to turn toward the front door.

"That isn't what I wanted to show you," Eve said as she reached into the shoulder bag hanging over the stairs banister and pulled out the rhinestone pin. She'd taken it out of her pocket because it kept biting into her flesh. Even dulled by years in the plane, the stones flashed, making her mother stop at the sight of the pin.

It was old-fashioned in its flower design and at least thirty-two years old, although Eve suspected it was much older than that. When she'd seen the pin in photographs, she'd always been fascinated by both the pin and the story her grandmother told with it.

As Eve held out the pin now, her mother seemed to shrink away. "What is that?"

"Don't you recognize it?" Eve asked, even though she could see her mother's shock at seeing the pin again.

Lila Bailey had recognized the piece of jewelry—just as Eve had done when she'd found it in the plane. "It's Grandma Nina

Mae's. The brooch Charley Cross gave her on their wedding day."

Her mother dragged her attention away from the pin and looked at Eve. "You're mistaken. It can't possibly be your grandmother's. She lost hers years ago, in Canada, I think she said. Anyway, there must be hundreds of pins around like it."

"Actually, I doubt hundreds of them have a replaced stone that doesn't quite match," Eve said. "I'm sure you remember the story."

Lila said nothing. She stood as if waiting for the next blow.

Eve wasn't sure why, but she suddenly felt sorry for her mother. Worse, she realized that she'd been angry with her for years and had blamed her mother for Chester moving out. She thought her mother cold, uncaring. And yet the woman standing before her looked sad and hurt.

Pocketing the rhinestone pin, Eve looked into her mother's eyes. She wanted to demand to know what her mother could possibly see in a man like Errol Wilson, but she couldn't bring herself to do it. She felt too weary.

"If that's all, I need to get back to my quilting," her mother said, and turned toward the door, walking quickly, seemingly afraid Eve would stop her. "We're working late tonight since…well, since we didn't get a lot done earlier."

Eve's fault. Eve always had been a problem, her mother's tone said. Now she was just making trouble again.

Eve couldn't help herself. "Don't you want to know where I found Grandma Nina Mae's pin?" she demanded as her mother opened the door.

Lila stopped in midstep, the door open, the chill of the rain wafting in. "Charley Cross broke your grandmother's heart. I doubt she would want a pin that would only remind her of him, do you?"

"Is that why there aren't any photographs of Dad in your house? Because he broke *your* heart?" she asked facetiously.

Her mother's fingers whitened as she gripped the doorknob. "I'm not having an affair with Errol Wilson. I'm sorry you misunderstood."

"Just as I misunderstood the letters I found under the floorboards in your sewing room?" Eve shot back.

"If you want to know why your father left, why don't you ask him." With that, her mother left, back ramrod straight, head high. But as Lila Bailey descended the porch stairs, her shoulders drooped. Eve saw her mother grab the railing to steady herself, stopping on the bottom step as if to catch her breath, head bowed.

That show of weakness lasted only moments. Quickly straightening, her mother walked briskly to her pickup through the rain, determination and resignation in her bearing.

As had constantly been the case, Eve felt drained from the exchange with her mother. She also felt sick to her stomach. Her mother had recognized the pin. And she hadn't even asked where Eve had found it.

Didn't it follow that her mother knew about the plane crash south of the ranch in the Breaks—and the murdered man inside?

GLEN WHITAKER HAD TRIED to hide his disappointment when the search party returned with the good news that Eve Bailey had been found alive and well.

Just as he'd suspected, no story here.

What a waste of time. Except for the pie. He'd stuffed himself on Arlene's pie and sampled all the other dishes as well. The only downside was Violet. She'd sat still as a stone, those watery eyes on him like a toad's on a fly.

Violet's younger sister Charlotte had joined them. The teenager smelled of artificial fingernail remover and had complained about being on her feet all day at one of the beauty shops in Whitehorse where she worked.

As Glen polished off the last of the pine-apple upside-down cake that Alice White had brought, Arlene said, "Glen, you and Violet should get together sometime."

Glen squirmed in his seat, trying to smile, wanting to run. "I'm pretty busy this time of year." A lie.

"Oh, you have time to take in a show or dinner out," Arlene pressed.

Glen scraped crumbs from his plate, eyes cast down. He couldn't bear to look at Violet, who'd made a pained sound at her mother's audacious efforts to pawn her off.

Charlotte was busy checking her long blond hair for split ends and obviously bored by the conversation.

"I'm busy, too," Violet said.

"I think the two of you would be perfect together," Arlene said, refusing to let it drop.

"Mama," Violet said on a breath.

The tension at the table was palpable. Glen felt a bad case of indigestion coming on. He'd stayed too long. He hadn't even noticed that it was getting dark outside. While skinny as a beanpole, he did love his food and he had to admit, the Old Town women were great cooks. But clearly, he'd worn out his welcome.

"Well, I really should get back," he said, rising from his chair. Violet had her head down, her neck flushed with embarrassment. Arlene looked disappointed and a little upset.

Glen felt guilty for eating most of the coconut-custard pie. "Violet, it was nice seeing you," he said, feeling he had to say something. "I'll give you a call." Another lie.

Violet lifted her head slowly. He felt a start when her eyes reached his. Fury. She knew he was lying. He thought her flush had been embarrassment, but now he realized it had been anger. And it was directed at him.

He hurried out, hating that he'd have to drive back in the dark. On top of that, it was raining.

Once he reached the car, he knew he was in no shape to drive home. He'd parked under a tree a ways from the center and now he laid back the seat and closed his eyes, just planning to let all that food settle before he headed home.

A sound woke him. He sat up, surprised to see that it was pitch dark and had stopped raining. A pickup pulled in and parked. He saw Lila Bailey get out. He'd seen her take food out to the sheriff earlier and then leave.

As late as it was, he was surprised she'd come back. But the lights were still on in the center and most of the old biddies' cars were still parked out front.

Just as Lila got out of her pickup, Errol Wilson materialized from the blackness along the side of the building. Glen, a born voyeur, watched with interest. It was clear they were arguing about something and that Errol had startled her.

Glen slid down a little, taking advantage of the darkness and the fact that they hadn't seen him sitting in his car. Surreptitiously inserting the key in the ignition, he lowered his electric window a little on the side closest to Lila's truck so he could hear.

Lila was keeping her voice down, but he could tell by her tone she was trying to persuade Errol Wilson of something.

A light breeze carried snatches of her voice on the chilly night air. Glen tried to imagine what the two could be arguing about and came up empty. After a moment, Errol grabbed Lila's arm, but she jerked free.

"You'd better do something about your daughter," Errol said angrily.

"I'm not putting up with you threatening me or my family anymore," Lila shot back with venom, advancing on him as she did.

Errol retreated a few steps, his movement awkward, as if he'd been drinking. Errol must have sensed they weren't alone. He glanced in Glen's direction.

Glen made a play of reaching into his pockets, as if looking for his keys. When he glanced back, the man was gone and the door of the community center was closing behind Lila Bailey.

What had that been about, Glen wondered as he reached for the key in the ignition. It was time to go home.

As he turned to look behind him before he pulled out, the driver's-side door of his car swung open. He felt the cold along with droplets of rain from off the car roof as he twisted around in surprise.

From out of the darkness came what felt like a bolt of lightning. Lights flashed behind his eyes. A thunderous sound echoed in his cranium. He felt the pain as he was struck in the head a second time.

The last thing he remembered was someone pushing him over, then the sound of his car engine, the crunch of the tires on the gravel and, as crazy as it seemed, the cloying scent of Violet Evans's perfume.

Chapter Seven

After her mother left, Eve sat down with the rhinestone pin cupped in her palms. The stones were cool to the touch. The metal was discolored. As many times as her grandmother had told her the story of the pin, Eve felt as if she was holding something priceless.

Grandma Nina Mae would pull Eve up on her lap and open her old photo album to the day she got married and say, "This is your grandfather, Charley Cross. He was a fine man, no matter what you hear about him. He never stopped loving me. This is the day we got married."

Nina's voice would soften. She would gently touch Grandfather Charley Cross's face and say nothing for a long time.

Then her grandmother would tell her about the pin that she always wore on her brown coat. "Your grandfather gave it to me. It meant everything to me."

"What happened to it?" Eve would always ask.

"Lost. It got lost. That's why you must always keep what you value close." And then her grandmother hugged her tightly.

As Eve studied the pin, she turned it over and saw something that she'd missed before. Several brown threads were caught in the backing of the pin.

She got up and found a sharp knife and worked the threads out of the base of the pin. The threads were frayed at the ends, indicating that the pin might have been torn off an article of clothing.

Her heart began to pound like a drum in her chest. They were threads from her grandmother's favorite old brown coat. If she'd had any doubt about whom the pin belonged to, she didn't anymore. If she had her grandmother's brown coat, she could prove it.

When her Grandmother Nina had gone into the nursing home, Eve had helped pack up all of her things. Her grandmother had saved *everything*. But Eve remembered the old brown wool coat her grandmother had worn until it was threadbare. Lila had tried to talk Nina Mae into getting rid of it, but her grandmother would have none of it.

"You throw out my favorite coat, Lila, and

I swear I will curse you until the day you die," Nina Mae had cried. "You know how much that old coat means to me."

"Mother, it's threadbare. I doubt it even fits you anymore," Lila had argued.

"It's mine," her grandmother had said, angry and hurt. "You of all people should know how much it means to me. I want to be buried in it. Eve, you make sure she buries me in that coat."

"I will, Grandma," Eve had promised.

Her mother had rolled her eyes at them both, but given up and stuffed the old coat deep in one of the trunks.

Eve felt her heart race. Grabbing a piece of clean tape, she carefully attached the threads of fabric to a scrap of paper, which she folded and put in her pocket along with the pin.

Now all she had to do was find the trunk her mother had put the coat in. The attic upstairs was empty. Eve had checked out the whole house when she'd moved in.

Was it possible her father had taken the trunks to the attic at the ranch? Or had Eve's mother gotten rid of them?

It wouldn't have been the first time. Eve Bailey had been eleven when she found the love letters hidden under the floorboards of her mother's sewing room.

She'd found them quite by accident. She'd

gone in to use her mother's good sewing scissors even though she knew she would get in trouble if she got caught.

She'd dropped the scissors, heard the odd sound they made as they struck the floor and, when she'd knelt down to retrieve them, she'd felt the floorboard move.

The letters were all addressed to "My Love" and signed simply "Your Love." It was in one of them that the man had asked whether Lila was ever planning to tell "the child" the truth. And Eve had known the truth had something to do with her—the duckling of the family.

And this man, Eve surmised, must be her mother's mystery lover—and probably Eve's *real* father. He would have dark hair and eyes and look like her. She had hungered for someone who resembled her.

She'd heard her mother coming and had quickly put the letters back under the floorboards, too shaken to confront her mother until she'd had time to think about what it all meant. Finding the letters had been a delicious secret that had kept Eve awake most of the night. She didn't want to give up that secret and she was positive that no one else but her mother and lover knew about the letters under the floorboards.

The next day, Eve had returned to the sewing room, intent on reading all the letters to see if she could figure out who the man was and what truth her mother hadn't told "the child." She fantasized that the man wasn't just her father but that for some mysterious honorable reason he had to remain a secret.

But the letters were gone, the space empty.

She'd confronted her mother only to have Lila tell her that she knew nothing about any old letters but if there had been some, they'd probably been in the house long before either of them was born.

Eve had cried and told her she knew Chester wasn't her real father. Lila had sent her to her room, saying she would hear no more of this foolishness and how she was never to say that ever again for it would deeply hurt Chester.

Without the letters, there was no proof. And Eve hadn't wanted to hurt Chester.

Nor could Eve ever be sure the letters really had been her mother's. Maybe there was no mystery father. Maybe Eve Bailey was just who her mother said she was, the firstborn of Lila and Chester Bailey. And the reason Eve had felt as if she didn't belong was because…well, because she was foolish, just like her mother had said.

Or maybe, Eve thought as she looked at the piece of costume jewelry, Lila Bailey had lied to her. Just as she had about the pin.

But then how much of the other had been lies as well? Had she lied about an affair with Errol Wilson? About the love letters under the floorboards? About Chester being Eve's father?

The pin was proof.

But proof of what?

IT GOT DARK FAST out in the Breaks. Carter had found a spot out of the wind, pitching his small one-man tent. The storm had moved on, but low clouds still hung over the stark landscape and the air was damp and cool.

He crawled into the tent fully clothed, leaving the door open. Night fell like a blanket when it came. There was no sign of a light, the darkness complete. No sound, either, other than the occasional rustle of his horse pastured off to the east or the cry of a hawk searching the canyons for food.

Carter lay on his back staring out through the open tent door at the sky, wishing at least for stars or even a sliver of moon to break free of the clouds. He'd spent many nights in the Breaks hunting. But tonight felt oddly different.

Probably because he knew he'd pay hell getting to sleep after everything that had happened today—seeing Eve Bailey again at the top of his list.

He was still amazed she'd come back. When he heard she'd been buying paint at the local hardware store and was living in her grandmother's house, he'd felt elated. Maybe she was staying.

Before that, he thought he'd never see her again except maybe at her wedding—if she had it in Whitehorse. Now, after seeing what she was doing with her grandmother's house, he wondered if she hadn't come home to stay.

Of course that begged the question why?

Was it just bad luck that she'd been home a couple weeks and discovered an airplane that had crashed in a ravine deep in the Breaks years ago?

He hated being suspicious. Especially of Eve. Deena had made him leery of women in general, but never Eve Bailey. Yet he couldn't explain the way Eve had been acting. Acting almost as if she was hiding something.

A sound. He stopped to listen hard, telling himself he was jumpy because he knew there was a body just over the lip of the ravine. Why else would he feel so vulnerable out here tonight? Hell, he had a weapon and no one knew he was out here.

Or did they?

He couldn't overlook the chance that whoever killed the passenger in the plane was still alive, still living close by. But Carter wondered if the killer must not have known where the plane was. If the craft had gone down in a blizzard in the middle of winter as he suspected, then if anyone had survived, they might not have been able to find the airplane again.

But the killer would know the plane was out here somewhere. After thirty-two years, though, he wouldn't expect anyone to find it. He'd—

This time the sound Carter had heard earlier was closer and he recognized it for what it was, the ring of a horse's hoof on a stone.

He slipped out of the tent, taking his flashlight and his weapon as he did. The night was so dark it was like being in a cave, but he didn't turn on the flashlight.

He'd been so sure that no one could have survived the plane crash, that the murderer had died trying to get to shelter, his bones scattered to the wind over the past thirty-two years.

But Carter knew if the killer had reached one of the ranch houses, then someone from this community would have had to have taken him in. And kept it a secret all these years.

The question was: how far would they go to keep that secret?

Another clink of a horseshoe against stone. The horse whinnied as the rider approached slowly, almost tentatively, and he realized the rider had to be tracking him using some sort of night glasses.

Carter moved to crouch just below the hill. Even with night goggles, the rider wouldn't be able to see him or his tent. With his horse a rise over, the approaching rider would be practically on top of Carter before he realized he was there.

He held his breath. There was always the chance it was just someone curious about what the sheriff was doing out here. Friend or foe? Wouldn't a friend have called out by now? But then the rider didn't know exactly where he was, right?

As Carter waited, the only sound was the slow click of the horse's hooves along the rocky terrain as the rider grew closer and closer.

Still, Carter couldn't see the horse or the rider. The night was too black. But he could hear both. He shifted the flashlight into his right hand, put his finger over the switch and silently urged the rider to come just a little closer. Carter wanted to see who'd tracked him out here.

The interloper's horse whinnied again. The sheriff's horse answered. All sound stopped.

Carter held his breath as he readied the flashlight. Just a little closer. He knew the moment he raised up to look over the crest of the hill, he would be a target. He'd be an even better target once he flipped on the flashlight to get a look at the rider.

The weapon felt awkward in his left hand, but he wasn't about to fire it unless forced to. If only the clouds would part. Even a little starlight might silhouette the rider—

Just a little closer.

The rider's horse whinnied and Carter's answered it again. The interloper quickly turned his horse and took off at a gallop the way he'd come.

Carter swore as he rose and flicked on the flashlight. The beam caught nothing but dust as the horse and rider raced away into the night. He swore as he stood listening to the sound of the horse's hooves die away in the distance.

If the rider was who Carter feared it was, then the murderer now knew that his secret was no longer safe.

VALLEY NURSING HOME was just outside of Whitehorse in a single-story red-brick building.

As Eve entered the next morning, she heard two women having an argument at the nurses' station. Both strident voices were easily recognizable, given that the two were usually arguing when Eve visited.

The large nurse had her hands on her hips, her face and voice calm as she stood between the two elderly women, trying to make peace.

One of the elderly women was tall and thick with slightly stooped shoulders, cropped gray hair and intense brown eyes.

The other was petite and ramrod straight with a gray braid down her slim back, startling blue eyes and an attitude that radiated around her like a high-voltage electrical field.

"Grandma Nina Mae," Eve said as she approached the latter woman's back.

"You're in for it now," Nina Mae said, without turning around. "My daughter is here and she'll settle this right as rain."

The nurse shot Eve a compassionate look. "It's your granddaughter Eve, Nina Mae."

"Don't you think I know my own daughter?" Nina Mae snapped, still not looking at Eve.

Eve reached for her grandmother's elbow, hoping to distract her. Nina Mae had her good days and bad. Today was obviously one of her bad ones.

Nina Mae jerked free to glare around the nurse at the other elderly woman, her once best friend—before a man had come into the picture. And long before old age and dementia had set in.

"You sneaky, underhanded—"

Eve got a better hold on her grandmother and steered her down the hall as the nurse took an irate Bertie Cavanaugh in the opposite direction.

"What's going on, Grandma?" Eve asked as Nina mumbled unintelligibly under her breath.

"Tried to steal him again. Thinks I don't know. A woman's husband isn't safe around here." She glanced at Eve and frowned. "You aren't my daughter."

"I'm your granddaughter Eve."

Nina didn't look as if she believed that, but clearly had other things on her mind. "That woman always wanted him, you know."

Eve knew. She'd heard the story enough

times over the years to recite it verbatim. Bertie and Nina Mae had been in love with the same man, Charley Cross. Nina had gotten him for more than thirty years of marriage, although he'd turned out to be no prize. And while Charley had taken off before Eve was born—and not with Bertie Cavanaugh—Nina Mae had never forgiven her friend for trying to steal Charley.

It amazed Eve that even at eighty-six, her grandmother still carried all the old grudges. Clearly time and advanced age didn't heal all wounds. And while her grandmother couldn't remember what had happened two seconds ago, parts of her past were as alive and real for her as if it were yesterday.

"That woman would steal the gold out of your teeth," Nina Mae grumbled as Eve steered her grandmother down the hall to her room and helped her into a chair.

Eve glanced around the room. "Where is your photo album?"

"You sound just like my daughter, Lila, but you don't look a thing like her."

"Isn't that the truth," Eve said, spying the photo album tucked under her grandmother's bed. She pulled it out, sat down on the bed and, her fingers trembling, began to leaf through it, looking for the photograph taken on her grandmother's wedding day.

Eve saw at once that some of the photographs were missing. "Where are your wedding pictures?" she asked her grandmother, who was fidgeting in her chair by the window. "Did you put them away somewhere?" It would be just like her to hide them.

Her grandmother raised her head and for a moment Eve thought she saw understanding in the older woman's eyes. "Who are you?"

"I'm Eve, Grandmother."

"Eve?" The name meant nothing to her. Just like the face. Eve couldn't imagine what it must be like to have chunks of your life, as well as people, erased as if they never existed—and yet her grandmother couldn't seem to forget that Bertie Cavanaugh had wronged her years ago.

Eve had wished for that kind of memory loss when Carter had broken her heart. Unfortunately...or maybe fortunately, she could remember quite well.

"She and that other one steals things."

"What other one?" Eve asked. But her grandmother's mind had moved on to a loose thread on the sleeve of her blouse.

Bereft, Eve watched her grandmother, remembering when she smelled of lilac and would envelop Eve in her arms, holding her in a cocoon of warmth and safety. Her house had smelled of warm bread and she would lift Eve up on the counter and slather butter onto a thick, rich piece and together they would eat the freshly baked bread and Grandma Nina would tell stories between bites as sunlight streamed in the window.

"Grandma?" Eve said, closing the photo album. The photos she remembered were gone. Either someone had taken them. Or her grandmother had hidden or, worse, destroyed them.

Eve reached into her pocket. "Have you ever seen this before?" She cradled the pin in the palm of her hand as she closely watched the elderly woman's expression.

Was there a flicker of recognition?

Nina Mae reached for the pin and took it in her arthritic fingers, turning it to brush her fingertips across each rhinestone, stopping on the one Charley Cross had replaced after her grandmother had lost the stone.

"You remember it," Eve said, her voice wavering.

Grandma Nina Mae's eyes filled with tears as she shoved the pin at Eve. "Get it away from me!" she screamed. "Get it away. Charley. Oh, my precious Charley."

Eve dropped the pin into her shoulder bag and tried to calm her grandmother, but Nina Mae was hysterical now, wailing and wringing her hands.

The nurse came running, demanding to know what had happened.

All Eve could do was shake her head. "Grandma. Grandma, I'm so sorry. I—"

"Please leave," the nurse said irritably. "Let me get her calmed down."

As Eve left the room, she was close to tears. The last thing she'd wanted to do was upset her grandmother. Her mother had been right. Grandma wanted to forget Charley. But did she also want to forget what had happened in that airplane? Because Eve had no doubt that her grandmother had not only recognized the pin—she'd been in that plane.

As Eve was leaving the building, she spied Bertie, both hands in her pockets, hunched protectively over the smock she wore as if hiding something.

Eve was reminded of her grandmother's accusation against Bertie. Was it possible Bertie had taken the photographs? The ones Eve remembered of her grandmother's wedding and the rhinestone pin she was wearing that day?

Or could it have been the other person her grandmother had referred to?

An alarm went off. Eve turned to see the nurse chase down one of the patients who was trying to escape through the side door. When Eve looked down the hall again, Bertie was gone.

Once outside, Eve headed for her pickup, upset with herself. She shouldn't have taken the pin from the plane. She should have told the sheriff about it. It was evidence in a murder investigation.

But Eve knew that was exactly why she'd taken it. For some unknown reason her grandmother's pin had been in that plane. Because her grandmother had been wearing it and her favorite brown coat? Thirty-two years ago her grandmother would have been young and healthy enough to walk away from the crash.

But where did the murdered man fit in?

Eve couldn't explain it but she had a feeling that the truth would force other secrets to come out. Ones she would wish had stayed buried.

Chapter Eight

Carter heard the whoop-whoop of the helicopter just moments before it rose up out of the Breaks.

He'd finally dropped off to sleep last night. It had taken a while. He hadn't been able to shake the feeling that the murderer had been out there in the dark last night. That he'd tracked Carter into the Breaks, afraid the sheriff had found the plane.

If the murderer had known where the plane had crashed, then he would have come back and disposed of the body years ago. But it made sense that if the plane had crashed in a blizzard in the middle of winter and the pilot and maybe one of two of the passengers, depending how many had been in the plane, had escaped, they would not necessarily have been able to find the plane again.

The plane had been too well hidden, the area remote. Few people ever went into this side of the river gorge. Hunters preferred the side with the pines. So did the elk and the large mule deer.

What scared him was that if he was right, the murderer now knew the plane had been found and would cover his tracks, if not disappear entirely.

Then again if it was someone who lived around here, that disappearance would be like a red flag. So there was a good chance that if the killer was local, he might stay put, blend in just as he had for the past thirty-two years, which would only make him harder to find. But none the less dangerous when cornered.

The chopper set down, the motor dying, blades slowing. The doors opened and three crime-lab techs jumped out.

"Mornin'," Carter said, extending a hand. He'd worked with one of the men, a man his age named Maximilian Roswell. Max shook hands with Carter and gave orders to the other men to get the gear ready.

"So what do we have?" Max asked, glancing down in the ravine.

Carter told him about the plane and the body

inside. "The last entry in the logbook was February seven, 1975."

Max let out a low whistle and nodded. "You said the body in the plane *mummified?* That's consistent with the entry in the logbook. If the plane went down in the middle of winter, the body would have kept well, drying out in the cockpit slowly as the weather eventually warmed. And you say the man inside the plane is a passenger. No sign of the pilot?"

"There's a chance the pilot didn't make it out of the Breaks."

"Would be hard to find any remains outside the plane after this long," Max said. "But then, too, he could have made it to one of the ranches."

"If he knew which direction to go," Carter agreed.

"Which could mean he was local. Or that he'd seen the ranches when he'd flown over before the storm hit."

Carter glanced down into the ravine. "What are the chances of identifying the victim?"

"You didn't find a wallet or any other identification?"

"No. I didn't want to disturb the crime scene any more than it had been," Carter said.

"What about prints? The person who found the plane climbed inside to get out of a storm."

Max pulled out his notebook. "And this person who found the plane?"

"Her name is Eve Bailey. She just moved back."

Max lifted a brow. "You know her then."

"Yeah," Carter said. "I know her."

AFTER EVE LEFT the nursing home, she stopped by the grocery store as was her usual routine. She never spent much time in Whitehorse, just in and out for supplies and back to the ranch. It had worked well since she'd been home. She hadn't run into Carter. No, that had taken her spending the night in the Breaks, she thought with a groan.

As she came out, a figure stepped from the shadows directly into her path. Startled, she hugged the paper sack of groceries to her and stopped so abruptly she turned her sore ankle again.

"Eve."

Her mind had been on Sheriff Carter Jackson, so she was even more startled to find his ex-wife Deena Turner Jackson standing in front of her, blocking her way.

"Deena." This was something else Eve had tried to avoid—an encounter with Deena.

"I see you found your way out of the Breaks," Deena said, an edge to her voice. "Didn't really need Carter to save you after all."

For the life of her, Eve had never understood the animosity Deena had toward her. Deena had gotten Carter. No contest. Eve hadn't even been in the running. So what was the woman's problem?

Just the sight of Deena brought it all back, though—the hurt, the heartbreak, the betrayal. This was the woman Carter had chosen over her. It was that simple in her mind, that painful to admit.

It didn't help that Deena was so beautiful. Eve had never seen her without makeup or with a hair out of place or wearing something that didn't flatter her.

Eve lived in jeans and always had. Unlike Deena, who had been born and raised in a city, Eve grew up on a ranch. Dresses were something to be worn to weddings, funerals and church.

Also, Eve usually had to pick up feed or fertilizer or some other ranch supply. It would have been pretty silly to dress in anything other than jeans and boots when she came to town.

And that was exactly what she was wearing today—jeans, boots, a Western shirt, her long dark hair in a ponytail, a straw hat pulled down to shade her eyes.

Deena Turner Jackson wore a sundress, sandals and had her blond hair swept up in the latest fashion.

"Is there something you wanted?" Eve asked, realizing that it was no accident their paths had crossed today. Deena must have seen her pickup and been waiting for her.

Around her neck Deena wore a gold chain with what appeared to be her wedding ring hanging from it. She touched the ring now as if it were a talisman, her eyes maybe a little too bright as she smiled at Eve.

Now what? Eve had heard about the divorce, just as she'd heard about the fights and the reconciliations over the years. For whatever reason, Carter and Deena just couldn't seem to stay together any more than they could stay apart.

"Don't get the wrong idea about me and Carter," Deena said.

Eve had no idea what the woman was talking about and said as much.

"There are things you don't know about him."

Eve was sure there were. "Nor do I care." She started to step past, but Deena blocked her way again.

"He isn't the man you think he is."

Eve laughed at that. "You have no idea what kind of man I think he is. Look, Deena, why would I care about Carter Jackson? Remember? He dumped me for you."

Deena brightened a little. "Yes, he did, didn't he?"

"Now if that's all," Eve said, not sure what she would do if Deena tried to block her way again. After all, she was a Bailey and if she hadn't had an armful of groceries…

"You will never have Carter."

Eve bristled. There was nothing she hated more than being told she couldn't have something. She would die trying to prove that person wrong.

Except that one time years ago. Deena had told everyone the very next day that she'd been with Carter. Once Eve had heard that, she wanted nothing to do with him. Carter had tried to call her a few times. She hadn't taken the calls and avoided him. She'd hidden her heartbreak, graduated and left town as fast as she could. Carter had betrayed her. She had wanted nothing to do with him.

But that was all water under the bridge now. And while she might regret that she hadn't given Deena the fight of her life for Carter, she wasn't going back down that road.

"I repeat, I don't want Carter Jackson," Eve said. "Now get out of my way."

Deena hesitated, but only a second before stepping back. "He will always be in love with me," she called after Eve. "He just used you."

Eve did her best to ignore the woman as she climbed into her pickup. She couldn't imagine anything worse than brawling over Carter Jackson in front of the grocery store, especially at this late date.

But at the same time, Eve had no intention of being that nice to Deena next time. And she was certain there would be a next time.

CARTER MADE a few calls on his way home to shower and change. He called in the identification numbers on the downed plane to the Federal Aviation Administration and was waiting to find out who it had belonged to.

He'd forgotten all about Deena until he pulled up in front of his place and saw the package waiting for him on his doorstep.

He hesitated as he started up the walk. The

large box was brown cardboard, with some kind of manufacturing printing on the side. He tried to remember if he'd ordered anything, wishing that was the case.

But he knew better. He'd married a woman he hadn't really known, brought her into his life with a wedding ring and a vow to love her until death parted them. He'd even given her his name—something he'd never get back. Just like the years he'd tried to make the marriage work.

Deena didn't love him. He doubted she ever had. Deena just didn't want anyone else to have him. It was crazy. Completely crazy. And scary. To have someone want you so much that they'd do *anything* to have you. It scared the hell out of him to even think how far she would go.

It reminded him of the time he'd seen a fox corner a mouse at the edge of a fence. The fox would give the mouse an escape route and even a head start before pouncing on it again.

He'd felt sorry for the mouse. Even as the mouse tired, it seemed to hold out hope that the next time it would get away. The fox finally accidentally killed the mouse. He watched the fox bat the dead mouse around.

Clearly, the fox was sorry he'd killed it, the game spoiled.

That's how he felt it would be with Deena. He'd thought he'd gotten away when he'd divorced her. But he knew that the only way she'd ever let him go was feetfirst.

Had he really thought that a legal piece of paper would deter Deena? So what was next? Having her arrested? He groaned at the thought.

She'd pulled on every heartstring she could think of on this quest to get him back, to revive the chase. Over the weeks, he'd found a lot of things on his doorstep, on his desk at work, even once before he'd changed the locks, inside his rented house.

Each time, he'd made the mistake of calling her to demand she stop. As a trained officer of the law, he knew about stalkers, knew that the worst thing you could do was respond, because that only encouraged them. It was just hard to see someone you'd loved become a stalker.

He'd known that if she hadn't stopped after being warned a half-dozen times, then a restraining order wasn't going to faze her.

He didn't know what it was going to take.

He stepped closer to the box, half-expecting to find it ticking. The top of the box hadn't been taped, the corners tucked under with only a dark hole at the center.

He considered what to do with it. He thought about calling one of his deputies to dispose of it. But he was so tired of Deena's pranks and presents.

Giving the box a wide berth, he opened his front door, glad to see that nothing seemed amiss. Not that this was any palace. He'd rented it after moving out of the house he'd bought when he and Deena had gotten married.

It was hard to believe that it had been almost two years and he was still living out of boxes.

He recalled Eve's place. She was trying to make the place her own. His house didn't even look lived-in, the walls a faded white just like they'd been when he'd moved in. He thought about the warm colors Eve had tried on the walls. Even with paint cans and cloths on the floor, the feel of her place had made him want to sit down in one of the overstuffed chairs by the window and stay.

He'd been tired for too long.

He stood for a moment, disgusted with himself. For months he had been stalled, unable to move forward, unable to go back.

But after seeing Eve today, he was ready to move on.

He showered, shaved, changed clothes and went to work, avoiding the box on his doorstep.

There were a half-dozen messages on his desk from the newspaper. Glen Whitaker probably wanted a quote. Carter balled up the slips and was about to toss them in the trash can when the dispatcher appeared in his doorway.

"It's Mark Sanders from the newspaper again," she said. "He's trying to find Glen Whitaker. No one has seen him since yesterday evening at the Whitehorse Community Center."

"He's probably just running late," Carter said, making a face. "You know Glen."

She nodded. "What do you want me to tell Mark?"

"That I'm checking into it," Carter said. "Thanks." He had no doubt that Glen Whitaker would show up and, meanwhile, Carter had something he needed to take care of first—a call he'd wanted to make the moment he saw the Navion plane in the ravine.

Loren Jackson answered his cell phone on the third ring. "Carter," his father said, his greeting more jovial than usual, which meant his father must be in his plane, although Carter couldn't hear the engine.

But high in the air seemed to be where Loren was the happiest. That certainly hadn't been the case when he was on the ground in Montana.

"How's Florida?" Carter asked. It was part of their usual ritual. Next they'd discuss the weather and fishing and after that Carter would hang up.

"I wouldn't know."

Carter frowned. Florida weather was either hot or wet or both. The fishing was either excellent or damned good. "What do you mean, you don't know?"

"Actually, I'm headed your way," Loren Jackson said.

His father hadn't mentioned a visit the last time they'd talked, which hadn't been more than a couple of weeks ago. In fact, the last time they'd talked, Carter had made a point of asking his father to come up to White-horse. It had been years since Loren had been back and Carter had only visited his father in Florida once and that was several years ago.

His father had seemed content enough in Florida, but Carter still thought it odd how quickly his father had left after losing his wife to cancer. Also strange was that there were no pictures of Carter's mother in the small beach house his father had bought. There were no pictures of any kind to document Loren Jackson's past except for his first airplane— a Cessna 172.

Apparently, his father hadn't just started over in Florida; he'd completely erased his past as if there was nothing about it he wanted to remember.

Why the sudden change of attitude now? A sliver of worry worked its way under Carter's skin at the thought of the person who'd ridden out to his campsite last night. He'd thought then that the secret was out. Was it possible the horseback rider had warned others?

"Is something wrong?" Carter asked his father now. "You're all right, aren't you?"

"I'm fine. Can't I just want to come visit you and your brother?"

Yeah, sure, maybe. Carter's suspicious mind was wondering if his father had heard about the plane being found. If that was the case, then his father's sudden appearance in Montana would mean that his father had some connection to that plane crash and the dead man inside.

Feeling scared at the thought, he asked,

"Dad, did you know anyone around White-horse who owned a Navion about thirty years ago?"

"A Navion?" his father repeated. "Listen, son, my cell phone battery is running low. Let me call you back when I get to town."

And just like that, his father was gone.

Carter swore under his breath. Just before Loren Jackson had disconnected Carter thought he heard a meadowlark in the background. But if true, then his father wasn't in his plane. He was already in town.

Either way, Carter felt his mistrust growing at an alarming rate. He wished Eve had never found that damn plane. But then, he suspected she wished the same thing.

Chapter Nine

Lila Bailey stood in her kitchen, staring into the refrigerator trying to remember why she'd opened the door to begin with. She was losing her mind. Just like her mother.

It had been like this ever since Eve had disappeared only to return with that ugly rhinestone pin, and now there was a story circulating that a crime-lab helicopter had been seen heading into the Breaks just south of the ranch, the same area Eve had been found yesterday.

Lila stared into the fridge, telling herself she should eat something because she had to get over to the community center and help finish Maddie Cavanaugh's quilt.

And yet she didn't move. She wasn't hungry. She felt numb and scared, and knew her problems with her oldest daughter had started almost from the time Eve was a baby.

Eve had always been difficult. Chester said it was because she was too smart for her britches. Lila suspected it was because Eve had a way of reading people. From the first time Lila held Eve in her arms and offered her a bottle, Eve had looked up at her with suspicion.

Lila had raised all three girls the same, loving them, caring for them, protecting them. If anything, she'd given Eve more love because she'd seemed to need it more than McKenna and Faith.

But maybe it hadn't been love Eve needed most. Lila could still remember the day she went upstairs to put some of the girls' clothing away and found Eve standing in front of the mirror, frowning. Eve couldn't have been more than five at the time.

"I look funny," Eve had said.

"Don't be silly. You're beautiful."

"Why isn't my hair the same color as yours and Daddy's?" she'd asked stubbornly.

Lila had turned away, busying herself with putting the clothing into the dresser drawers. "Because God blessed you with dark hair and eyes. He wanted you to be special."

Eve hadn't bought it. "I don't want to be special."

Lila had turned then to look at Eve. "We're all special. Like snowflakes, no two the same."

Eve's intent eyes had bored into her. "Violet Evans said I didn't belong to you and Daddy. She said I was *adopted*. What's adopted?"

"Violet Evans is a...silly goose. I don't want you listening to a thing she says." Lila wanted to wring Violet's neck. The girl must have overheard her mother spreading gossip.

It wounded Lila that Violet could do something so mean. Lila intended to have a word with Violet's mother. She knew Arlene was just jealous. Eve was such a beautiful child. Violet was plain and gangly like her mother.

"Now go outside and play," Lila had ordered Eve, and walked out of the room.

But Eve being Eve, it hadn't ended there.

"Lila?"

She whirled around at the sound of her name, at the familiar and yet painful sound of it on his tongue and stared in shock at the man standing in her kitchen.

It had been so many years and yet it felt as if it had only been yesterday.

He stepped past her to close the fridge door, brushing her shoulder as he did.

She felt a jolt of electricity shoot through her, leaving her weak and trembling. "Loren."

"I knocked but no one answered," he said, studying her now. He looked so large in her big roomy kitchen. But then Loren Jackson had always taken up too much space around her. "I came right from the airport."

"What are you doing here?" Her voice was raspy, sounding like she felt. Close to tears.

She wanted to throw herself into his arms, remembering the feel of being wrapped up in him, needing him now more than he could imagine.

"I just heard that Chester moved out," he said. "I'm sorry. Are you all right?"

Sometimes she forgot Chester was still alive, still her husband. For her, he was neither.

"I'm fine," she said, the worst kind of lie.

She stared at the man she'd once loved more than life. Loren Jackson had changed. He was tan, his hair completely gray but cut short, making him look distinguished. He was still a large man, broad in the shoulders. Still devastatingly handsome.

She thought of his son, Carter. Handsome like his father. In fact, Carter resembled Loren when Loren was that age. She felt a flush of shame remembering the day she had caught Carter and Eve kissing. The jealousy she'd felt. Lila had been relieved when they'd broken up. It was better for her not seeing Carter, not remembering his father.

"You shouldn't have come," she said, turning away from Loren now.

"You had to know I would."

She grabbed the edge of the kitchen counter. No, she hadn't known he would. A part of her believed she would never see him again, hoped she wouldn't.

"Lila, why didn't you let me know the moment Chester left?" he asked behind her.

She shook her head. Because it was too late. It had been too late the moment Loren married Rachel Hanson.

Loren came around until he stood so close she could feel goose bumps rise on her arms. Her heart threatened to burst at even the thought that he might touch her.

And then he did, his hands cupping her shoulders. She felt the shock, then the warmth, then the comfort that she'd craved since the first time Loren Jackson had brushed his lips over hers, the first time he'd made love to her. She leaned into him as if coming home.

"Lila, you need me. Don't send me away again."

"Mother?"

Lila jerked back at the sound of Faith's voice. At the shocked, reproachful tone of it.

"Mr. Jackson?" Faith said as Loren let go of Lila and turned around. Faith sounded both surprised and upset to see him, but then she'd always been Chester's favorite. Of the three girls, Faith had taken it the hardest when Chester moved out.

"Mr. Jackson stopped by looking for Carter," Lila said.

Faith's gaze narrowed. "I didn't see the sheriff's patrol car when I pulled in."

"Carter is probably down at Eve's," Lila said.

"I should go," Loren said, obviously feeling the same chill in the room that Lila now did. He stepped past Faith, giving her a nod just as he'd done Lila and then he was gone. Again.

Lila stared after him, trembling inside, intensely aware of the gnawing ache that seemed to be eating away the last of her sanity.

Faith gave her a disgusted look as she passed. "I would expect better of you, Mother."

Lila couldn't imagine why, as her daughter stomped up the stairs just as she'd done as a child. Chester would have gone after her, tried to soothe her.

But Lila moved to the window to watch Loren Jackson drive away, her emptiness so complete she felt as if she were weightless. Like this morning's rumors about the body found in a plane in the Breaks. Nothing left but a mummified skeleton. Everything that had made it human lost long ago.

UPSET OVER THE PHONE CALL to his father, Carter drove down to the Milk River. The sun lolled high in a cloudless blue sky, making the air hot and dry. Crickets chirped from the bushes as Carter pulled up. His radio squawked. It was the call from the FAA.

"I have that information you asked for on the Navion," the man said.

Carter listened, then thanked him and got out of the patrol car. Opening the door to the bait shop, he found his brother in the back filling the minnow tank.

Cade Jackson looked up but didn't say anything as he continued working. Cade was the older, taller and more pigheaded of the two brothers. But he was also the most solid, both of his feet firmly planted in Montana, stable as granite.

Like Carter, his hair was dark, his eyes a deep brown. Women had always flirted abashedly with Cade.

But there had been only one woman for his brother. Carter wondered if it ran in the family.

"Well?" Cade asked, without turning around. "I wondered how long it would take before you came by."

"You heard Dad's coming to town?" Maybe already in town.

"Yep. He called earlier. He said he'd see me later today."

That was so like their father to call Cade, but not him. "He say what he's doing here? I mean don't you think it's a little strange?"

"Didn't say and no I don't think it's any stranger than Eve Bailey getting lost in the Breaks and you having to rescue her," Cade said, humor in his voice.

It had never dawned on Carter that anyone might think Eve had spent the night in the Breaks just to get his attention. "Eve wouldn't do that." Deena would, if she'd have thought of it.

"She's a woman and so far it isn't apparent why she's back in town," Cade joked.

Carter groaned. "Trust me, I'm the last guy on earth she wanted to find her."

Cade turned from the tank to look at him. "So it's true? You never got over her."

"I didn't come in here to talk about Eve Bailey," Carter snapped, making his brother laugh. "I need to ask you something."

Cade turned off the water, wiped his wet hands on a towel and gave his brother his undivided attention.

"Did you ever hear Dad or Gramps talk about a four-seater Navion going down in the Breaks?"

Cade blinked. "That's what you have to ask me? You sounded so serious, I thought—" He stopped abruptly. "Damn, did you find the plane?"

"Eve did, but it's under investigation, so I need you to keep it under your hat for the time being," Carter said, knowing he could trust his brother. Also knowing the news was probably already spreading faster than a wildfire, with the crime-scene helicopter flying over Whitehorse and Old Town this morning.

"I remember a few planes, but none that weren't found." Cade was watching him. "What kind of investigation?"

"Criminal. There's a body still in the plane. Looks like the guy was murdered."

Cade swore. "But what does this have to do with Dad? He hasn't even lived here for—"

"The plane's been there for thirty-two years apparently," Carter said. "You got to admit, it's odd. The plane is found and not twenty-four hours later Dad flies in."

"You're not thinking Dad was the pilot," Cade said.

"There weren't that many pilots around this area thirty-two years ago. Especially ones who had their own airstrip—the closest airstrip to the crash."

"The pilot probably wasn't local."

"The plane was. I just got the call from FAA. It belonged to a guy from Glasgow."

"So how could that have anything to do with Dad or Gramps?" Cade demanded.

"Thirty-two years ago, the owner had been dead for two years," Carter said. "The plane had been stored in a hangar at the airport. The man's wife went to sell the plane only to find out it was gone."

Cade shook his head. "Come on, you think Dad or Gramps stole some guy's plane? Why would they do that? They both had their own planes."

Carter could think of several reasons they would do that. "Dad and Gramps would have known about a Navion sitting in a hangar in Glasgow. They would also have heard that the guy was dead and the plane wasn't being used."

Cade rolled his eyes. "Circumstantial evidence at best."

"Come on, you know as well as I do that their crop dusters didn't go as fast and weren't as durable as an aluminum plane. Not to mention their planes were too well-known in the area."

"You're saying they had some reason not to want to be recognized?" Cade swore. "You think the plane was carrying some sort of contraband?" He scoffed. "If they didn't want to attract attention, they'd have used their own planes. No one would think anything of one of the Jacksons' planes landing on the Jackson ranch airstrip."

He had a point.

"But then I'd have to believe that Dad or Gramps were killers," Cade scoffed.

Carter had been a sheriff long enough to know that anyone could kill under certain circumstances.

"This is crazy."

Carter agreed. This was crazy. "We'll know more when we find out who the victim was. The crime-lab techs are getting the body out now. With Dad probably already in town, I just have a bad feeling about this."

"Like Dad could keep some deep dark secret all these years." Cade turned back to his minnows. "You really should take up fishing again. You need an outlet other than cops and robbers."

And murderers.

Back in his patrol car, Carter reached for his squawking radio.

"Mark Sanders is on the phone again," the dispatcher said, and Carter groaned inwardly. "Glen Whitaker didn't show for his interview. His car isn't at his apartment and no one has seen him since he left the Whitehorse Community Center yesterday evening."

Carter cursed under his breath. "Tell Mark I'm on my way out to Old Town. I'll keep an eye out for him." As he started the patrol SUV, he told himself he needed to go down there anyway. He had to see Eve.

EVE BAILEY GLANCED at her watch, relieved to see it was the time her mother left to go to the community center to quilt. McKenna and

Faith were at work in town and had plans to go to the play in Fort Peck. They wouldn't be home until late tonight.

In the barn, Eve saddled her horse, more than grateful to the mare. She credited the horse with saving her life. If the mare hadn't returned to the ranch, no one would have known she was missing and Eve was pretty sure she would have never made it back to the ranch on foot yesterday. Last night, she'd been so exhausted, she'd fallen to sleep the moment her head touched the pillow.

As she worked, she grudgingly gave some of the credit for her rescue to Carter Jackson. She hated to think what would have happened if he hadn't found her yesterday. If no one had. That was big country. They could have missed her easily enough.

She tried to tell herself that Carter had just been doing his job. Thoughts of him turned to thoughts of Deena and the run-in with her. Eve wanted nothing to do with either of them.

Carter and Deena had broken up more times than Eve had even heard about, she was sure. But they always got back together. No reason to think they wouldn't this time. Even with the divorce. Eve planned to give them both a wide berth, just as she'd been doing since she'd been home.

As she finished cinching up the saddle, she suddenly had the strangest sensation that she was being watched. Turning, she looked toward the road. Something flashed like sunlight on glass. She blinked. Whatever it had been it was gone. Odd.

She swung up into the saddle, anxious to go for a ride—even only as far as her mother's house. Carter crowded her thoughts again like an unwelcome conscience and she knew as long as she had the rhinestone pin she'd taken from the plane, she wouldn't be able not to think of him.

Heading east, she rode out across the prairie. She made a wide circle, enjoying the ride, and came out behind the ranch house in a stand of trees. As she reined in, she saw her mother leaving in her pickup.

Eve waited until the dust had died down before she dismounted and headed for the house. No one would be back for a long while, but she felt the need to hurry. She knew it was foolish, but she didn't want to get caught up in the old attic searching for her grandmother's favorite brown coat. If the coat was even still there.

Mostly, she hadn't made up her mind what she would do with the coat if she found it and if the threads from the pin matched. Getting caught would only force her into a decision.

She feared her mother would have already gotten rid of the coat—right after Eve had showed her the pin. Unless her mother had forgotten where the coat was stored.

Eve slipped in the side door of the house that had been her home the first eighteen years of her life. The smell alone brought back good memories. She felt guilty for her suspicions as she moved quickly toward the back stairs.

The old wooden stairs creaked under her step. The house felt strange. Too empty. Even the air had an odd feel to it, as if the house had been abandoned and no one lived here anymore.

Once on the second floor, Eve opened the small door to the attic. It groaned loudly, startling her. She thought she heard a vehicle approaching, froze to listen, but then heard nothing.

Why was she so spooked? But she knew the answer to that. She'd been scared ever since she'd seen that body in the plane, seen the knife sticking out of the man's chest and found her grandmother's rhinestone pin on the floor at the man's feet.

Eve left the door open to let out the musty air of the attic and climbed up the narrow creaking stairs. At the top, she felt around until she found the light switch and snapped it on. Hurriedly she looked around the attic for the old wooden trunk her mother had put the coat in.

The trunk had been at Grandma's house, but Eve's father must have moved it up here after Nina Mae went into the nursing home.

The attic was full of furniture, lamps, even an old crib that Eve and her sisters had slept in. Her mother hadn't thrown anything away apparently.

Eve spied the big wooden trunk in a back corner and worked her way to it. Brushing off cobwebs, she bent down and lifted the lid. The trunk hinges groaned loudly. Eve stopped again to listen. No sound but the pounding of her heart.

Hurriedly, she searched the trunk. The coat wasn't there. She rummaged through the old clothing a second time and realized she'd missed the coat because she'd remembered it as being more substantial than it was.

The coat was just as her mother had said:

threadbare. It had been rolled up in a bottom corner—right where her mother had put it.

Eve drew it out with trembling fingers, praying she was wrong as she spread the coat over her lap. She checked one lapel, then the other. In the dim light of the attic, she missed the hole the first time.

The threads had been broken from the spot on the lapel where the pin had been in the photograph Eve remembered. The hole was jagged—as if the pin had been torn from the lapel. She pulled out the threads she'd taken from the pin and compared them. They were a perfect match!

Tears rushed Eve's eyes as she gripped the coat in her hands, fear washing over her. Didn't this prove her grandmother had been in that plane?

A door opened and closed downstairs. Eve rushed to the small dirty window and looked out. She couldn't see a vehicle nor had she heard one since earlier, but she knew someone was here.

Her mother? Had Lila returned for some reason? Or one of her sisters? Eve felt a chill as she remembered that her grandmother hadn't been the only one in the crashed plane. Along with the dead man, there'd been a pilot. Maybe even another passenger. And one of them was a murderer who could still be alive.

Eve's heart raced as she looked around for a place to hide her and the coat. She heard footfalls on the stairs. No time. Someone was headed upstairs.

The light. Belatedly, she reached for the pull cord and turned it off. Had her mother returned and seen the light on in the attic from the road?

She remembered she'd left the attic door open. Whoever was coming up would see that it was open.

She was trapped.

She quickly stuffed her grandmother's coat behind a chest of drawers, then looked around for a place to hide herself. The tall highboy. She could hear footfalls on the attic stairs, the tread too heavy to be her mother's or one of her sister's. The killer? She recalled that feeling of being watched earlier and knew even before she heard him stop, the top stair creaking, that he'd followed her here and knew she was alone.

Chapter Ten

Carter heard a soft rustle deep in the attic. "Hello? Eve?"

She let out a groan that sounded both relieved and angry as her head appeared from behind a tall bureau.

"You scared me half to death," she snapped.

"I scared *you?* Why didn't you answer when I called from downstairs?"

"I didn't hear you."

"What are you doing up here?" he asked as he glanced past her to where she'd been hiding.

"Looking for a lamp for my house," she said a little too quickly. "Not that it's any of your business."

He raised a brow. "Really? In the dark? And I would have thought you'd have driven your pickup over if you were planning to pick up a lamp instead of riding your horse."

"Are you spying on me?" she demanded as he snapped on the light.

"As a matter of fact, I drove down to make sure you were all right. I was worried when I saw you ride off again so I followed you on foot. This lamp you're after, it must be valuable. Otherwise, why wait for your mother to leave before you sneaked up here to get it?"

"I didn't sneak."

It was clear to him that she hadn't wanted anyone to know she was here. Now why was that, he wondered as he noticed a large old wooden trunk, the lid up, the clothes inside it appearing recently rummaged through.

"What's going on, Eve?" he asked seriously. "After everything you went through yesterday, why the urgency to get a lamp out of—" He stopped as he heard a vehicle engine followed shortly by the slamming of a car door.

Eve heard it, too. He saw the fear in her eyes. What the hell was going on?

Her attention darted to the old trunk with the lid standing open.

As he heard the front door open and close and footfalls cross the hardwood floor, he reached over and closed the trunk lid and saw relief in Eve's expression.

She hurried to snap off the light an instant before he pulled her back behind the high bureau where she'd been hiding before and whispered, "Did I mention I saw your mother head for your house? I think she was looking for you."

He felt rather than saw her reaction. She seemed to hold her breath and listen, just as he was doing as they hunkered behind the highboy.

The footsteps seemed to hesitate at the bottom of the attic stairs. Whoever it was had seen the open attic door, just as he had. A moment later, the attic steps groaned.

He waited. He could feel Eve doing the same.

The last stair creaked, then the light snapped on and footfalls moved across the floor.

Carter peered around the end of the highboy to see Lila Bailey drop to her knees in front of the old wooden trunk, the same one that he'd just closed.

He glanced over at Eve. She had leaned to the edge of the highboy and was now watching her mother. She didn't seem surprised as the trunk lid groaned open.

Lila began to dig frantically through the trunk, then slammed the lid with a curse. "Oh, Eve, what have you done?" she cried. Then she did the last thing Carter expected. Lila put her head down on her arms on the top of the trunk and began to sob.

Carter felt Eve's hand on his arm as if she wanted to go to her mother. But then she removed it and stayed behind the bureau with him until her mother's sobs subsided. Lila dried her eyes, turned out the light and went back down the stairs, shutting the attic door behind her.

It wasn't until Carter heard Lila drive away that he stepped out from behind the bureau and turned on the light, his focus going to Eve. "What *have* you done, Eve?" He could see that she was shaken after what she'd witnessed. "Eve, talk to me."

IT WAS HIS SOFT TONE that was Eve's undoing. She couldn't pretend that he didn't know her. Or she, him. Nor could she go on carrying this burden alone.

Slowly, she reached into her pocket. She'd wrapped the pin in a flowered handkerchief that she'd found in her grandmother's house. It smelled of lavender.

She could feel Carter watching with

interest as she carefully pulled back the tatted edges of the kerchief to expose the rhinestone pin.

"It belonged to my grandmother," she said.

Carter held out his hand and frowned as she dropped it into his palm.

"It was a present from my grandfather, Charley Cross," Eve said. "Grandma Nina Mae wore it on her brown coat at her wedding. She never took it off the coat. She told me that when she lost it, just like when she lost Charley, she never got over it."

"Eve, what does this have to do with—"

"Her pin…" Eve's throat tightened, her heart aching at even the thought of what she was about to do. She wished she'd never found the plane. Never found the pin. Never recognized it. She swallowed, thinking about her grandmother. "I found her pin on the plane."

He stared down at the piece of jewelry in surprise. "You found this on the downed plane in the Breaks?"

She nodded, close to tears.

"How can you be sure it's your grandmother's?" he asked, the ramifications of what she was saying obviously finally hitting home.

"A few days before my grandparents got

married, Grandma lost one of the rhinestones out of the pin." Eve had heard the story a thousand times so she knew it by heart, but she stumbled over the words. "Nina Mae was just sick about it. So my grandfather took the pin and, even though it was only costume jewelry, had a jeweler in Great Falls put another stone in. If you look closely you can tell which one it was. The stone never quite matched because it's a diamond."

"Eve, slow down. This doesn't prove…" His eyes widened. "There's more." He let out a curse. "Of course there's more."

She brushed at an errant tear, miserable. "Grandma always wore the pin on her favorite brown coat. Both were in all the old wedding photographs. I found brown fibers on the back of the pin. I checked them. They match. There's also a hole in the lapel where the pin had been torn free."

He glanced at the trunk. "That's what your mother was looking for?"

She nodded.

Carter took a breath and let it out slowly. "Eve, do you know what you're saying here?"

She chewed at her cheek, feeling as if she'd just betrayed not only her grandmother, but her entire family. Her grandmother would never know, but her mother...

Eve was still shaken after seeing her mother cry the way she had. It had taken everything in Eve not to go to her. But she knew that Lila would be horrified to know there had been witnesses to her breakdown.

Her mother's reaction to not finding the coat in the trunk pretty much told the rest of the story. Lila Bailey, the queen of secret-keepers.

Yes, Eve thought, she knew exactly what she was saying. Not only was her grandmother on that plane, but her mother knew about it and had kept Grandma Nina Mae's secret all these years.

That's why Eve hadn't told Carter about the pin the morning he found her in the Breaks. Because she'd feared that if her grandmother had been on that plane, then someone in her family had to have known. And her grandmother knew not only the victim, but also the killer.

"Eve, a man was murdered," Carter said. "There is no statute of limitations on murder. Also, there is a law, as you well know, about withholding evidence."

"I had to be sure it was Grandma's."

"You said there are photographs of your grandmother wearing the coat and pin?"

She hated to tell him. "The photos seem to have disappeared."

He swore. "And you don't know anything about what happened to them."

"No, I don't," she snapped. Not that she could blame him for not believing her. She'd kept the information about the pin from him. And might have kept the coat from him as well. Just as she hadn't told him about showing the pin to her mother.

One betrayal per day was enough.

CARTER WAS STUNNED. He had suspected Eve was withholding information from him, but he'd never dreamed it might be something like this.

To make matters worse, if she was right and her grandmother had been on that plane, then they might never know the truth—at least not from Nina Mae Cross.

Nina Mae had Alzheimer's. Whatever her role was in all this, it was lost somewhere in her deteriorating mind.

"Who knew you'd found the pin in the plane?" he asked.

Eve hesitated, but only for a moment. "I didn't tell anyone about the plane."

"But you showed your grandmother the pin."

She nodded, looking contrite. "At first she just seemed so happy to see it again, but then she became hysterical and wanted nothing to do with it."

Carter shook his head. "I wish you'd told me about this."

The answer was in her eyes. She hadn't trusted him. Given their history, he couldn't blame her.

And yet she had told him about the pin. True, he had her cornered in an attic, but maybe she was starting to trust him again.

"So the coat was in the trunk," he said, recalling Lila Bailey's reaction to not finding what she was looking for. So Lila knew about the pin as well. Did it follow that she knew about the plane? And the murdered man?

How many others around here knew and had kept the secret? He hated to think.

He looked at Eve and wanted to take her in his arms and hold her. He would do anything to protect her from what he feared would come out of this investigation. She looked pale and scared. He knew the feeling.

"Even if your grandmother was on the

plane, she didn't kill that man and we both know it. Where is the coat?"

Eve stepped behind a chest of drawers and pulled out the rolled-up brown cloth. With obvious reluctance, she handed it to him.

"The coat is threadbare, but my grandmother's wish was to be buried in it—"

"I'll make sure you get it and the pin back," he said.

"What happens now?"

"I'll have to hang on to both as evidence, Eve," he said, not any happier about that than she was. He'd known Nina Mae Cross and her daughter Lila Bailey all his life.

"I'd like to be alone now," she said.

He didn't want to leave her, but he had no choice. As far as he knew, the reporter Glen Whitaker was still missing and he needed to talk to Lila Bailey.

"Eve, be careful. Whoever killed that man in the plane…well, the murderer might not have gone very far thirty-two years ago. Not very far at all."

Sick at heart, Eve rode her horse home only to find a note from her mother.

Eve,
I have to attend a funeral in Great Falls.

I'm not sure when I'll be back. Please don't do anything until I return. We need to talk,
Mom.

A funeral in Great Falls. Eve didn't believe it for a moment. Her mother had taken off knowing questions would be demanded of her.

Eve opened all the windows as if fresh air would chase away the fear, the anger, the concern for both her grandmother and her mother.

The curtains billowed in the breeze. The day smelled of new grass and sunshine and, soon, the usual—paint.

She had changed into her paint clothes, needing to do physical labor, needing to forget everything that had happened since she'd come home.

But as she stood in the middle of the room, paint brush in hand, she had that odd sense again of being watched.

She moved to the edge of the window and looked down the dirt road. The grass grew tall on both sides. She could hear crickets chirping, smell fresh-cut hay, see birds teetering on the phone lines overhead.

There was no sign of anyone spying on her, and yet she couldn't shake the feeling.

Worse, as she turned her attention back to the mess in the living room, she couldn't remember why she'd even started this project. She hadn't planned to stay. She'd only intended to remain here until she had satisfied the questions she had in her mind. Fixing up her grandmother's house had been just something to keep her busy until she could get to her real reason for coming home.

And that reason had been to find herself. For as long as she could remember, she'd been restless. Isn't that why she'd believed there was some secret involving her?

It had been a series of things that made her still believe that. How different she looked from the rest of her family. Finding those mysterious letters under her mother's sewing room floorboards that mentioned "the child." The feeling that she had another family somewhere.

She'd come home convinced that the answer was here and that she'd never be happy until she found out the truth.

Now all she wanted to do was leave. To run. She was good at running. Bad at staying and fighting for what she wanted. Only she'd never wanted to run as badly as she did right now.

She picked up the can of paint and climbed the ladder. She couldn't run. Not this time. She'd come home to put some matters to rest, including what was going on with her parents. Finding the crashed plane in the Breaks, well, she'd gotten more than she'd bargained for, because that had brought Carter Jackson into her life again—and left her with even more questions about her family.

She shivered and opened the can of paint. After dipping in the brush, she made a wide swipe of color across the wall, then leaned back a little to consider it.

The paint was a warm orange shade that complemented the woodwork. It reminded her of sunsets down in the Breaks, when the horizon appeared to be on fire. Color would shoot up into the sky. Pinks and reds and pale yellows.

Her mother would hate the orange. That alone should have made it perfect. Eve just couldn't make up her mind. She was edgy, worried, afraid. All the things she'd been that had forced her to come back here.

She leaned against the ladder, thinking about her mother slumped over the trunk sobbing as if her heart were breaking. But it was her mother's words she heard now echoing in her thoughts: *"Eve, what have you done?"*

What *had* she done?

The phone rang. She put down her paintbrush and went into the kitchen, brushing an errant lock of her hair back from her face as she picked up the phone. "Hello?"

"Eve?"

"Dad." She couldn't believe how glad she was to hear his voice right now.

"I was wondering if you wanted to come up to Whitehorse for dinner?" Chester Bailey asked, sounding shy and unsure. "I have the day off and I thought…"

Eve felt a drowning wave of guilt. She hadn't seen him since she'd come back, although she had talked to him a couple of times on the phone. "Sure, I'd love to," she said, even though driving to Whitehorse was the last thing she wanted to do.

She looked down at her paint clothes. "It could take me a while."

"No problem. I'll meet you at the Hi-Line Café."

AFTER DRIVING a few back roads, but having no luck finding the missing reporter, Carter returned to his office hoping there would have been word.

While Glen Whitaker hadn't turned up, Carter did find his father waiting for him in his office.

Loren Jackson fidgeted in one of the chairs opposite his son's desk. He didn't seem to hear the door open, giving Carter a moment to study his father.

Loren Jackson was television-rancher handsome. He was a man who'd always been larger than life, tanned and looking healthy as a horse.

But there was also something about him that made Carter uneasy. His father was clearly nervous. What had made him fly in so unexpectedly and right after a crashed plane had been found in the Breaks? Something was up with Loren Jackson and Carter had a bad feeling he knew what it was.

"Dad," he said, stepping the rest of the way into the room. "Just couldn't stay away any longer, huh?"

Loren Jackson stood as Carter held out his hand. The two clasped hands for a moment before Loren pulled him into a quick hug. "It's good to see you, son."

"You, too, Dad." Carter stepped behind his

desk, wishing he hadn't noticed that the notes on his desk that he'd taken regarding the plane in the Breaks had been moved. "You just get homesick for Montana?"

His father nodded, but gave no explanation for what he was doing here. "You look good. They keeping you busy?"

Idle chitchat?

Carter leaned back in his chair. "What's going on, Dad?"

His father gave him a confused look and shook his head. "Can't I come see my favorite son?"

"Cade is your favorite son," Carter said, only half joking. "Find anything interesting in my notes?" he asked.

Loren shook his head slowly, giving up all pretense.

"Why the interest?"

"You know me and planes."

"Yeah, I do. I also know there's more than a good chance that you knew the pilot."

"Oh? You've found him, then?" Loren asked, sounding surprised.

"Not yet, but I will."

"After all this time, does it really matter?"

Carter stared at his father in surprise.

"Yeah. As I'm sure you read in my notes, a murdered man was found in the plane."

Loren Jackson said nothing.

"Why don't you tell me what *you* know about it," Carter suggested.

"Me?"

"You going to also tell me you didn't know a pilot from Glasgow who owned a Navion?" Carter pressed. "Couldn't have been many Navions within an hour's drive from White-horse."

"What was the pilot's name?"

"Herman 'Buzz' Westlake," Carter said patiently, knowing his father probably knew far more than he did about this whole affair.

"Buzz, sure, I knew him," Loren said.

"You ever fly his plane?"

Loren thought about that for a few moments as if deciding what answer might be best. "You know I think I did. Buzz took me up once. Let me take the controls. Nice plane."

Carter could see he was getting nowhere. "Dad, if you know something—"

"Son," Loren said, getting to his feet. "I just came home to see you and your brother. It had been too long. This plane being found…well, it's just too bad. You'll have everyone looking at their neighbors, suspecting each other. No good can come from this. Hell, boy, it was years ago. Who cares?"

"I do. Someone got away with murder. That someone might still be living around here."

His father frowned. "Not very dangerous, since apparently he hasn't killed anyone since." Loren Jackson moved to the door and stopped, turning back to face his son. "You've seldom listened to any advice I've given you. This is the one time you really should. What's past is past. Let this one slide. It's best for everyone involved."

Carter couldn't believe what he was hearing. "In case it's slipped your mind, I'm the sheriff. I'm paid to uphold the law. I don't let some murders slide. No matter how old they are. Or who's involved."

"That's too bad, son. Because I'm afraid you'll end up hurting the people you care about the most." With that, he turned and left, leaving Carter fearing the same thing.

CHESTER BAILEY LOOKED UP as Eve walked into the café, his face instantly lighting up at the sight of her and making her feel all the more guilty for not making a point of seeing him sooner.

"Eve," he said, getting to his feet to fold her in his arms. "It's so good to see you." He held her tight for a moment, then stepped back to look into her face and saw her tears. "Is something wrong?"

She shook her head. "It's just so great to see you." For years her only visits had been quick ones, little more than overnight and she was gone again.

Eve had come home, against her mother's protests, and moved into her Grandma's little house since it was sitting empty.

"What would you want with that old house?" her mother had demanded.

"The house has a lot of possibilities."

"Oh, Eve, you have no business back here. There are no possibilities for a woman your age," her mother had said.

"What is it you're so afraid of?" Eve had asked. "Why would my coming back threaten you so much, Mother?"

"Don't be ridiculous," Lila had snapped. "I just don't want this life for you. Your sisters are only home for the summer. I can't imagine what would bring you back here."

"Can't you?" Eve had asked.

"You settling into your grandmother's

house all right?" her father asked now, as he motioned to the booth.

"Yes, thank you," she said as she slid into the booth across from her father. He seemed smaller than she remembered, his shoulders a little more stooped, his hair much grayer and yet as he smiled across the table at her, he looked incredibly boylike.

"It's what your grandmother would have wanted," Chester said, then frowned as if wondering why she'd wanted the house, why she'd come back. "I'm glad you came home."

"I thought Mother might need me," she said, stumbling a little over the lie. "And you. How are you?"

"Just fine." He picked up his menu. "The special is chicken-fried steak, but have anything you want. Susie makes a fine fried boneless trout."

Susie? Just then a blond woman came out of the kitchen. She was small and slim, her face tanned and lined. Eve realized Susie had to be about her father's age.

"This is my daughter, Eve," Chester said.

Susie smiled at once. "Eve. I've heard so much about you. Your father is so proud of you. Maybe you could give me some tips on how to make this place look better," she said with a laugh.

"Susie just bought the café," Chester said. "I told her how you majored in interior design."

Eve nodded, sensing how close her father and Susie had become. "The place looks great," was all she managed to say. "I'll take some iced tea and the special," she said, without looking at the menu.

"I'll take the same," he said, smiling up at Susie as he handed her both menus.

The door tinkled behind them and Hugh Arneson from the lumberyard came in. "Eve," he called, "glad to hear you made it out all right."

Chester's smile faded a little as he waved to Hugh and asked Eve what that was about.

"I spent the night in the Breaks," she said. "A storm came in. It was just stupid on my part."

Her father's eyes widened. "When the hell did that happen?"

"Night before last. But I'm fine, really."

"I can't believe this is the first I'm hearing about this." He sighed. "I've been putting in a lot of hours at work. I didn't even get down to Whitehorse until today so I guess that explains it. But I would have thought your mother would have tried to reach me."

"It wasn't necessary," Eve said, covering

for her mother and wondering why. She lowered her voice. "Dad, what happened between you and Mom?"

He looked immediately uncomfortable. "Nothing happened. It's just easier living up here with me working in Saco."

Eve shook her head and looked out the café window. A half-dozen dirty pickups were parked along Main Street from the hardware store to the newspaper office.

"Honey," her dad said, reaching over to cover her hand with his. "Your mother and I just need a little time alone."

"Then you aren't getting a divorce," Eve asked in a whisper, her voice cracking with emotion. She hadn't realized until that moment how much she didn't want them to divorce.

"No, of course we aren't getting divorced," Chester said, then looked even more uncomfortable as Susie appeared to place two tall glasses of iced tea on the table. Susie had heard what he'd said. Her cheeks flamed with color and she quickly excused herself.

Eve had trouble catching her breath. Clearly her father was seeing Susie and at least Susie had thought Chester and Lila were getting a divorce. Eve took a long drink of the iced tea, knowing she wouldn't be able to eat a bite of her dinner.

Some more locals entered the café, all coming over to tell Eve how glad they were that she was all right. She thanked them, seeing that her father was getting more upset by the moment.

"I still can't understand why your mother didn't call me," he said.

Well, she's been kind of busy with another man. That and running off to funerals in Great Falls.

Did her father know about Errol Wilson? Is that why he'd moved out?

It dawned on Eve that she hadn't seen her mother take any clothing when she left the house earlier. Had her mother just come up with the funeral in Great Falls after she'd found the brown coat missing? Or had she gone to the Whitehorse Sewing Circle, then planned to pick up clothing for the funeral and leave? And was Errol Wilson going with her?

Their dinners came and they ate, making small talk about Old Town and Whitehorse. Eve managed to choke down some of her meal. The rest she moved around her plate until her father was through with his.

"I should get going," Eve said. "I want to

stop by and see Grandma before I go home. Thank you for dinner."

"Let's do it again. Soon."

She nodded and rose to leave. "Take care of yourself," she said as he rose and gave her a hug.

He nodded, his attention following Susie as she went to a table of some local men.

"If you get down to the ranch, you should come see what I'm doing with the house," she said.

He nodded distractedly. "I don't get down that way much anymore."

AFTER HIS FATHER LEFT, Carter sat in his office wondering if a child ever knew his parent. It was late, but he wasn't ready to go home. He'd never thought of his old man as someone who harbored secrets. But now Carter felt he'd only touched the tip of the iceberg when it came to Loren Jackson.

The thought scared him more than he wanted to admit.

Had his father tried to warn him off this case because he was the pilot of that plane? Thirty-two years ago his father would have only been twenty-four. Loren Jackson could have been flying that plane.

But so could his father, Martin "Ace" Jackson, who'd flown in WWII. So who was his father trying to protect? Himself? Or Ace?

Carter swore. Did he really believe that his father or grandfather could be murderers?

He picked up the phone and called to see if either of the deputies had had any luck finding Glen Whitaker. Neither had. Carter just hoped that nothing had happened to the newspaper reporter.

At the sound of a footfall, he looked up to find Maximilian Roswell standing in his doorway holding a large plastic container.

"Evidence from the plane," Max said, and stepped in, kicking the door closed behind him as he set the container on one of the chairs across from Carter's desk.

Carter felt a moment of panic as he stood and watched Max slide open the container, revealing at least a dozen evidence bags. "You might want to sit down, Sheriff. What I have to show you could come as a shock."

Chapter Eleven

Glen Whitaker came to in a barrow pit with the taste of coconut in his mouth. He was cold and confused, his legs weak, his head aching.

He managed to stumble to his feet. The landscape was flat and went on forever. He had no idea where he was.

But he could see his car in the opposite ditch, the front fender crumpled around a wood fence post.

He swore and tried to remember wrecking his car and couldn't. He took a step, surprised by how feeble he felt. His hand went to his forehead and he touched the double goose egg where he must have smacked his head on something when he hit the fence post. His body ached all over as if he'd been beaten.

Is that why he couldn't remember anything?

He stood, dizzy and dazed, and realized the last thing he remembered was waking up in his bed and wanting pancakes. When was that? This morning? Or yesterday morning? He stared at the horizon. If the sunset was any indication, he'd lost an entire day. Maybe more.

As he headed for his car, hoping it would at least get him to the nearest ranch house, he grimaced at the taste of coconut in his mouth and the smell of too-sweet perfume on his shirt.

What had happened to him?

THE NURSE STOPPED Eve as she entered the rest home. "It took us an hour to calm your grandmother down after you left. Whatever the problem was, let's not have a repeat of it this evening."

Eve promised she wouldn't upset her. But as she started down the hallway to Nina Mae's room, she wondered if she could keep that promise. Maybe just the sight of her would set her grandmother off again.

As she came around the corner of the hallway, she saw a man coming out of Nina Mae's room. He had a photograph in his hand and was looking at it. He must have heard Eve's approach, because he quickly turned, pocketing the photograph as he did and went out the side door, setting off the alarm.

Several of the nurses came running. Eve realized she hadn't moved. She'd been too caught up in wondering why he was in her grandmother's room—and trying to place him.

He was tall, nice looking with dark hair and eyes. She'd seen him before, but she couldn't recall where.

And then it came to her.

Bridger Duvall. He was the man who was renting the McAllister Place in Old Town. The mystery man.

At her grandmother's door, Eve stopped and looked in. Nina Mae's photo album was open on her lap and, even from the doorway, Eve could see a white spot on the page where another one of the photos was missing.

Did Bridger Duvall know her grandmother? Would Nina Mae have given him a photograph?

Her grandmother closed her eyes, the photo album sliding off her lap and hitting the floor. Nina Mae didn't stir.

Eve stepped in and picked up the album, studying the photos on the page where the latest one was missing. With a start she saw that the other three snapshots on the page were of her grandmother and her when she was a baby.

What would Bridger Duvall want with a photo of her and Nina Mae? As far as she knew he didn't know anyone in the area. But then why had he rented a house here?

Nina Mae opened her eyes.

"Grandma Nina Mae," Eve said, closing the album and kneeling down beside her grandmother's chair. She felt horrible for upsetting her earlier. "How are you doing?"

"Who are you?" she demanded peevishly.

This was so hard. Eve put her head down, bone weary. What had made her think coming home would give her peace? She ached all over and wished she was anywhere but here right now.

"I'm Eve, your granddaughter. I know, I don't look anything like you," she said, before Nina Mae could.

"Of course you don't look like me," her grandmother snapped. "You're adopted."

Eve froze. "What did you say?"

Her grandmother didn't answer.

Eve raised her head slowly. Nina Mae's expression had softened. She reached out with a hand and gently touched Eve's cheek, her fingers cool and smooth. Tears sprang to

Eve's eyes. "You remember me, don't you?" she whispered.

Nina Mae smiled, then closed her eyes and leaned back in the chair again. "Of course I remember you."

Her sisters had told her that Grandma Nina Mae sometimes had lucid moments. Was it possible this was one of them? "I was adopted. That's why I don't look like any of you, why I feel so restless and incomplete, isn't it, Grandma."

"How should I know?" her grandmother answered without opening her eyes.

"Because you're my grandmother."

"You have me mixed up with someone else. Don't you think I'd know my own grandmother?"

She'd said grand*mother.* Not grand*daughter.*

Eve rested her head against the arm of Nina Mae's chair, fighting tears. Her grandmother didn't know what she was talking about.

"She called earlier, you know," Nina Mae said.

"Who?" Eve asked.

"Grandmother. She asked when I was coming to see her. I told her I couldn't come for a while. I'm needed here."

Eve felt goose bumps dimple her skin. The

nurses said elderly patients often discussed talking to deceased relatives about going home just before they died. Eve didn't want to lose her grandmother. But then she'd already lost her, hadn't she?

She patted Nina Mae's hand until she fell back to sleep and began to snore softly. Rising, Eve looked down at her grandmother and felt a chill, although the room was uncomfortably hot. Eve had been convinced moments ago that her grandmother knew her, knew what she was saying.

Just like those few moments when Nina Mae had held the rhinestone pin her husband Charley Cross had given her so many years ago. Eve had seen the look on her face. She'd recognized the pin and had been remembering the good times connected with it. At least for a while.

Of course the pin would also come with bad memories, given that Charley had run off and left her.

She had so many questions, and now Grandma Nina Mae could no longer provide the answers. Eve had waited too long.

Wasn't it possible that Nina Mae spoke the truth without even realizing it? As a young girl, Eve had been convinced she was adopted. But, according to her birth certificate, she was born on February 5, 1975, at home. The local doctor, Dr. Holloway, had driven down from White-horse in a blizzard to deliver her.

With a start she remembered the date she'd found in the logbook from the crashed airplane. February 7, 1975. Just two days later.

On the way home, Eve got behind a rancher moving his tractor down the road to another field. She'd forgotten what it was like having farm implements on the highways, as well as ranchers often moving livestock in the middle of the road. But she hadn't forgotten this slower-paced life or that she'd missed it. She'd missed home, and that surprised her. Missed the people, the place.

She thought of Carter. His divorce from Deena had nothing to do with her coming home. Nothing. He'd go back to Deena. He always had. She shoved him out of her thoughts.

Too bad she couldn't do the same with the airplane she'd discovered in the gulch. Or the rhinestone pin. Or the fact that she believed her grandmother had been in that plane.

She thought of Bridger Duvall. She'd have to tell Carter about seeing him at the rest home. She was positive he'd taken the photo from Nina Mae's album.

But why would he want a photograph of Grandma and her? It creeped her out that if she was right, Bridger Duvall had a photo of her as a baby.

Her head hurt from trying to understand what was going on. She'd planned to ask her father some questions, but the café had gotten too crowded and her father had been so... different.

She had a flash of the way he'd smiled up at Susie. Her heart spasmed at the realization that her father might be happier where he was now than on the ranch with her mother.

Had he found out about Lila and Errol? Is that why he'd left? Eve hadn't been able to bring herself to ask. She didn't want to be the one to tell him if he didn't know. Maybe, more to the point, she knew her father wouldn't feel comfortable discussing it with her. He was a private man who kept things to himself.

Like her mother. And her grandmother.

CARTER TOOK the small evidence bag Max Roswell handed him, his gaze locked on what was inside. "This was in the plane?"

The hairbrush was small. A baby's. The handle was yellow, the hair caught in the soft white bristles dark and resembling goose down.

Carter looked from the brush to Max. "You aren't trying to tell me that…"

"There was a baby on board," Max said as he took a seat across from Carter. "We also found what was left of a cloth diaper, a dirty cloth diaper."

Carter groaned. "The baby couldn't have survived the crash."

"Depends on if the baby was strapped in some kind of carrying device. From the way the backseat belt was hooked up, I'd say the baby just might have been." Max pulled another evidence bag from the plastic container and handed it across the desk to him.

The small tube inside the bag was tarnished, but as Carter turned the bag in his fingers, he could still read what was printed on the bottom of the tube: Scarlet Red.

"Lipstick?" he said, his attention shooting from the tarnished tube to Max. "You think there was a woman on board as well?" He tried to sound surprised, but all he could think about was the rhinestone pin and the story Eve had told him about finding it in the plane.

"A woman *and* a baby," Max said.

Was it possible Eve was right about her

grandmother being on the plane. But a baby? "You really think they could have survived? It was the middle of the winter, the closest ranch house miles away."

"I would imagine someone was meeting the plane," Max said.

"But there is no place to land in the Breaks—" Carter stopped, aware of Max's focus on him.

"The supposition is that the aircraft got off course," Max said. "But not ten miles off course. This plane wasn't headed for the Whitehorse airport."

Carter knew where Max was going with this and decided to beat him to the punch. "You think he was headed for the airstrip south of my family's ranch? But in February?"

"I checked. It was a mild winter. There wouldn't have been much snow and when I flew over that old airstrip on the way here, I noticed that it's along a ridgeline. Snow would probably blow off anyway. I would imagine that's why your father and grandfather put the airstrip there to begin with, don't you think?"

Carter could say nothing as he recalled his conversation earlier with his father.

"A snowstorm blew in late on the afternoon

of February seven, 1975, a real blizzard," Max was saying. "I think that's when the plane went down. Missed the airstrip and ended up in that ravine."

"You're sure it was February seven, 1975?"

Max nodded. "I found a gas receipt stamped with that date. It was faded, but still legible."

Carter was having trouble breathing. He waited, afraid Max was about to tell him a Jackson had been flying that plane.

"We found something else in the plane," Max said, not sounding pleased to have to tell Carter this. "Evidence that drugs were being transported on the plane."

Drugs? Carter stared at Max, uncomprehending. A woman and baby *and* drugs were on the plane? No way was Eve's grandmother involved in drugs. Nina Mae had always been outspoken, opinionated and danced to her own drummer, but she was straight-as-an-arrow moral. She wouldn't abide drugs, let alone help transport and sell them.

Nor would his father or grandfather be involved in running drugs.

"Just because the plane might have been headed for my family's airstrip doesn't mean they were involved," Carter said with more heat than needed.

"No," Max said. "It doesn't. But it's a good bet someone in your family knew the plane was planning to land there. I'm not saying they knew anything about the drugs. The woman and baby would have made good cover for bringing in the marijuana." Max rose to his feet. "So it's just a matter of finding out if the pilot and the woman and baby survived and where they are now."

Carter stared at the investigator. "You can't seriously expect me to continue with this case. I'm too personally involved."

"Are you?" Max asked. "As you pointed out, we don't know that your family knew anything about it."

"But even if that's the case, there's a good chance I know the people who are involved. If you're right and someone was meeting the plane, the chances are it was someone local."

Max rubbed the back of his neck. "That's any small town. I know you, Sheriff Jackson, by reputation. You're not going to let personal feelings keep you from getting justice for that murdered man."

Carter wished he could be as sure of that as Max.

"There's some other evidence in the box you might want to take a look at," Max said.

"I'll let you know what we find out about your victim once we get him to the lab."

EVE WENT HOME and changed into her paint clothes, determined to decide on a color for the living room. Right now she had three walls painted three different colors.

The problem was, she couldn't quit thinking about what her grandmother had said about her being adopted. It had been so strange to hear her grandmother say something that Eve had suspected since she was old enough to notice that she didn't look like she belonged to this family.

She opened the orange paint can and stared down at the semigloss. This house was never going to get painted. She had to know the truth. It's why she'd come home. She'd had this stupid idea that her mother would be honest with her now that she was no longer a child.

But her mother hadn't been honest with her about anything. Not about Chester. Or Errol. Or the rhinestone pin.

No, if Eve wanted to learn the truth, she'd have to do it on her own. She picked up the lid to the paint can, and hammered it back on. Changing out of her paint clothes, she dressed in the darkest clothing she had as the little voice in the back of her head tried unsuccessfully to talk her out of what she planned to do.

What she needed was proof one way or the other—and not a birth certificate from her mother's doctor. If Eve had been lied to all her life, then her mother wasn't the only one who'd been in on it, she thought, as she drove back toward Whitehorse.

It was late by the time she reached the city limits and late enough that there was hardly any traffic. The usual pickups in front of the bars along the main drag, but no cars near the small building that housed Dr. Holloway's office.

Eve made a pass through town. The sheriff's patrol SUV was still parked in front of his office. She just hoped Dr. Holloway wasn't working late as well.

As she neared the doctor's office building, she slowed. No lights on. There were no other lights on in the buildings around it. Everyone had gone home for the day.

She parked three blocks away, picked up the cloth bag with the tools she would need and walked back to the doctor's office building using the dark alleys. Whitehorse was only about ten blocks square to begin with, so it was a short walk.

Dr. Holloway's office was the only one in the small building. There were no outside lights in the rear. The alley was pitch-black and a minefield of mud puddles and toe-stubbing rocks. She couldn't see her hand in front of her face as she stumbled toward the rear of the building, feeling like the criminal she was about to become.

She knew from all the times she'd come to Dr. Holloway's as a child that the files were stored in the basement. Doc, as he was commonly known, had to be hugging seventy by now and hated computers so refused to have one in his office.

Eve was surprised he hadn't retired. But since he often took vegetables in lieu of cash for his services, maybe he couldn't afford to retire.

The back door was old, just like the lock. Eve stuck the crowbar between the jamb and the door and put her weight into it. The weathered wood cracked so loudly Eve feared the sheriff could hear it in his office blocks away.

The door's edge finally splintered, exposing the interior of the lock. All she had to do was stick the screwdriver into the lock and turn.

The door opened and she stepped inside, closing it behind her, tallying in her head the cost of a new door and lock, restitution for breaking and entering. Doc had always told her she was his favorite Bailey girl, although Eve suspected he said the same thing to each of her sisters.

If she found what she suspected she would, there was more than a good chance Dr. Holloway wouldn't press charges. Otherwise, she'd have to throw herself on the mercy of the court.

Turning on the small penlight from her bag, she shone it down the stairs toward the basement door.

She wasn't surprised to find that the door to the basement was unlocked, but she was thankful.

In the basement, she swung the small penlight beam around the room, looking for a window. There didn't appear to be one so she turned on the light. The large room was full of boxes of nondrug medical supplies and boxes of who knows what. Doc got his drugs from the hospital so he kept little in the office. What few he did, he kept locked up in his safe upstairs.

Eve didn't see any medical records and for a moment feared he stored them elsewhere.

At the back of the room she spotted another door, this one marked Archives.

Hurrying to it, she tried the knob. Locked. She swore under her breath, that feeling of getting in deeper making her hesitate. In for a penny, in for a pound. Wasn't that how it went?

The lock on the archives room was a little harder to get open, but she finally managed to break it. She glanced at her watch, surprised twenty minutes had gone by.

The archives room was musty and claustro-phobic. As she stepped in, the door closed behind her, making her jump. She shoved at the door, terrified she'd just locked herself in.

But the door swung open without any trouble. She gulped the not-great basement air, then propped the archives-room door open with one of the boxes and searched for a light. The moment she flipped the switch, the lightbulb made a popping sound and the room went dark.

"Great." Eve turned on her penlight again.

The ceiling was low in there, the shelves and boxes stacked to the top. There were numerous rows of shelves with only a narrow walkway between each.

As Eve moved deeper into the room, she noticed that there didn't seem to be any rhyme or reason for the way the boxes had been arranged. "Would have been too easy to have filed them by last name," she muttered to herself as she moved down the stacks.

Apparently a number had been assigned to each patient. Eve swore again. Unless she had the codes, she'd never be able to find anything down here.

But then she realized that at the very back, the patient files had been stored by year. She found the year of her birth, then narrowed it down to the month. February 1975.

There was one huge box on the top shelf marked February 1975. She shone the light around, looking for something to stand on, and saw a small stool.

Dragging it over, she put the end of the penlight between her teeth and climbed up to pull down the box.

The box was heavier than it looked and she almost toppled off the stool. She dropped it. The box hit the floor hard, tipped and dumped a dozen files onto the cold concrete.

She thought she heard a sound overhead and froze, listening. She could hear the steady drip of a faucet somewhere overhead, but nothing else.

Hurry.

She scurried to pick up the files, using the penlight to search for her name or her mother's among them.

No Eve Bailey. But she saw one for Nina Mae Cross. Treatment for a broken leg. Her grandmother had broken her leg? Eve had never heard anything about that. Then Eve saw the date on her grandmother's medical record. *February 7, 1975.* The same date the plane had crashed in the Breaks? The time on the report was eleven at night! She scanned Doc's scrawl. Apparently it had been a hairline fracture. He'd splinted the leg at her grandmother's house.

Eve stared at the report. Did this mean what she thought it did? That her grandmother had broken her leg in the plane crash? But then Nina Mae wouldn't have been able to get out. Unless she'd broken it later, after she'd gotten out of the plane and the ravine.

Eve put the file aside, determined to find one of her own. That's when she saw a file for Mrs. Chester Bailey.

Eve opened the file and scanned it. The word "infertility" leaped out at her. She slowed to read as best she could what Dr. Holloway had written in his illegible scrawl. Apparently Lila and Chester had been trying to get pregnant, but with no luck. Doc had suggested infertility testing. Lila said she would talk to Chester.

Eve double-checked the date on the box, her heart pounding. Maybe the doctor's visit had been misfiled. If her mother had given birth to her February 5, 1975, then she wouldn't have been talking to the doctor about infertility tests any time in February of that year.

The office visit was February 2, 1975. She stared at it, knowing she shouldn't have been surprised, let alone stunned.

Her mother had lied. Eve didn't want to believe that her mother had lied to her again. How many secrets did her mother have, anyway?

Eve clutched the file to her. She finally had proof. With this staring her in the face, her mother would have to tell her the truth now.

Eve thought she would feel more elated than she did. She'd been right. But instead of elation, she felt numb. She really wasn't the child of Chester and Lila Bailey. No wonder she'd always felt different. Incomplete. Never felt as if she belonged. So who did she belong to?

She set the file down on the floor and

reached to pick up the box to put it back. It was too heavy. She was going to have to leave it. It wasn't as if the doctor wouldn't know someone had been here, given that she'd destroyed two of his locks. She planned to call him in the morning, anyway. With the file, she thought she finally might be able to get the truth one way or another. It hadn't slipped her mind that Dr. Holloway had signed her birth certificate which attested that she'd been born to Lila and Chester Bailey on February 5, 1975. Doc had been in on the cover-up. But why? Why hadn't they just told her she was adopted? It made no sense.

Eve couldn't wait to show her mother the doctor's file. Too bad her mother was at a funeral in Great Falls. Eve would have to wait until Lila Bailey returned.

She had started out the archives door when she heard a thud overhead. No mistaking it for a leaky faucet. Someone was up there.

Eve hurriedly turned off the light and tiptoed up the stairs to the back door. She could hear someone headed toward the back of the building. Any moment the door from upstairs would open and she would be seen.

She couldn't get caught. Not with the file. There was no way whoever was coming would let her take this confidential file. And she feared the file might disappear. Her first real evidence.

She ran for the back door just as the door from upstairs opened in a rush. All she saw was a large dark shape. He lunged for her. Without thinking of the consequences, she swung her sack of tools, catching him in the jaw. He missed the bottom step, thrown off by the blow, and tumbled down the short stretch of basement stairs to crash into a stack of cardboard boxes. She caught the smell of aftershave.

Eve flipped on the light, afraid she'd killed Doc Holloway, although it wasn't his usual brand of aftershave. But it wasn't Doc who looked up at her from where he'd landed on the floor.

Bridger Duvall. The same man she'd seen coming out of her grandmother's room at the nursing home.

Chapter Twelve

Lila Bailey had planned to be gone long before this. She stood at the window, staring out into the darkness. She'd only returned to the house to get some clothing. Unfortunately, her daughters' plans had changed and both McKenna and Faith were there.

Both girls had viewed her announcement with skepticism. Lila knew that they had discussed Loren Jackson's earlier visit and didn't believe her story about a funeral in Great Falls.

"Mom, it's too late to drive to Great Falls tonight," McKenna said as Faith came downstairs dressed for the dance they'd decided to go to in Whitehorse.

"Whose funeral is it, anyway?" Faith asked.

"A woman doctor friend," she said noncommittally. "You don't know her. And I prefer driving at night. It's cooler," she said to McKenna. "I'll be fine. You know when you girls are away at college I manage just fine on my own."

"Only because you choose to," Faith said.

"You don't have to go to Great Falls alone," McKenna said. "I could talk to Dad—"

"No," Lila said too sharply. "Thank you," she said, softening her words. "But your father didn't even know the woman and he has to work tomorrow." She knew her daughters worried about her. She wished they wouldn't. It only made it harder.

"I know Dad would come back if you asked him," McKenna said.

Even if true, it was the last thing she wanted. "This is between me and Chester."

McKenna looked disappointed, maybe even a little hurt. Lila squeezed her hand and looked past her at Faith. Her youngest daughter's expression chilled her to the bone.

"She doesn't want him back," Faith said angrily. "She's glad to be rid of him." With that, Faith went out the front door, slamming it behind her.

McKenna looked at her mother. "Is that true?"

"Of course not. He's your father. The last thing I want is a divorce." Not even that was true.

McKenna gave her a hug. "I know he loves you."

Lila could only nod.

She stood for a long time after the girls left, listening to the emptiness of the house to the beat of her own heart like a drum. Or a ticking time bomb.

She was just tired, she told herself as she headed for her bedroom to pack. Eve would show up next. She had to leave before that. She couldn't face Eve. Not tonight.

A warm wind billowed the curtains and she could smell the flowers the girls had planted outside her window. Tonight the sweet scent made her a little sick.

The house was two stories, a huge rambling thing that had belonged to Chester's family and been added on each generation. She'd loved the history in the worn wood floors, in the china that had been passed down for generations. All she'd ever wanted was to live in Old Town with the man she loved and have his children.

Lila scoffed at how foolish she'd been to think that could have ever happened. Life was full of disappointments. She'd planned to fill this house with children, male children who would someday take over the place.

Chester had been even more disappointed and disappointing. But she couldn't blame him. He'd known he wasn't her first choice any more than she'd been his.

She turned on the light in her bedroom, surprised how dark it had gotten. Time seemed to slip away from her, minutes lost in thought, hours gone as if stolen.

She heard the front door open. Maybe the girls had forgotten something and had come back. She reminded herself that they weren't girls anymore. "McKenna?"

No answer.

"Eve?" She knew Faith wouldn't have come back, as angry as she'd been.

Loren? He would have knocked. Or said something by now.

Lila turned and listened, her bedroom door open, the faint wash of light spilling across the floor from the small light she always left on in the hallway for when her daughters returned.

The front door closed with a soft click.

Lila froze, her heart lodging in her throat. She couldn't have screamed even if she'd tried. Even if it would have done any good. The closest house was Eve's and it was a half mile up the road. No one would hear her.

She heard the creak of a floorboard, then another before the groan of a heavy tread on the stairs. She willed her body to move. Across the carpet to the bed. Her hand trembled as she quietly opened the bedside-table drawer where Chester kept the .22 pistol.

"One shot wouldn't stop much of anything," Chester had said. "So you'll have to keep firing. Aim for the body. The main thing to remember is that if someone were to break in, if you don't stop him, he'll end up using your gun on you. That's why most men would never tell their wives to go for the gun." He had hesitated. "But you're not most wives."

No, she thought, she'd definitely proved that.

She flipped off the safety and raised the gun, her focus on the open bedroom doorway. She knew there would be that split second when the doorway filled and she would have to make the decision whether to fire.

It could be a neighbor. Or one of the girls. Or Chester. Someone who either hadn't heard her call to them. Or didn't care to answer.

Or it could be a drifter like the one who'd come through back in the 1970s, killed Margaret O'Dell in her bed and stolen her car to make a run for Canada.

A shadow fell over the doorway an instant before the bulk of a man filled the space.

Her finger tightened on the trigger as Errol Wilson stepped in.

He smiled when he saw the gun. "That's what I love about you, Lila. You have such a sense for the dramatic."

She itched to pull the trigger and wondered why she hadn't the first time he'd come into her house with his threats.

But she knew the answer to that.

"Get out."

Errol leaned suggestively against the doorjamb and grinned at her.

"I said get out."

He arched a brow at her. "Don't make a mistake you'll regret the rest of your life, Lila. I've waited long enough."

"I told Chester."

"Chester?" He laughed as he stepped toward her. "Even if I believed you, I know Chester isn't the person you've been hiding the truth from all these years."

"My girls are women now. They'll understand."

Errol must have heard the fear in her voice. He chuckled. He was now within feet of her. Her heart pounded so hard she barely heard him, but the gun never wavered in her hand.

"We both know who you're protecting, Lila, and just how far you will go to keep your secret," he said. He was close enough now that she could see the lust in his eyes.

"If you don't leave now, I'll pull the trigger."

"Yeah, right," Errol said, grinning. "Explain my dead body to your family and friends."

She caught her breath as he snatched the gun from her and snapped the safety on before tossing it onto the bed.

"Come on, Lila, you know this day has been coming for a long time. I would hate to have to force you, but I will."

Lila Bailey clamped her mouth closed to keep from screaming as she felt Errol Wilson's wet lips on her neck. She caught sight of the gun lying on the bed.

He shoved her down on the bed, grinning as he began to unbutton his shirt. She'd run him off last time when Eve had seen him leaving. Just as she'd run him off before. But she knew nothing would stop him tonight.

He opened his shirt. She stared at his bare chest as he started to lower himself onto her, his belt buckle cutting into her stomach. Reaching up to the corner of the bed, she found the gun. It would be so easy to kill him.

She thought of her daughters, especially Eve, as her fingers tightened around the barrel of the gun. Errol was kissing her neck, so sure she would have to give into him now that Chester was gone, now that Eve was home again. He never saw it coming as she swung the gun as hard as she could at his balding head.

The base of the grip connected with the back of his skull, the sound like dropping a cantaloupe on concrete. He'd known she wouldn't shoot him. But she saw that he hadn't expected this. He drew back to look at her in both surprise and pain.

She shoved him off. He tumbled off the bed, landing hard in a sitting position staring up at her, breathing hard.

"I told you to get out," Lila said.

He blinked at her, having a hard time focusing while he reached to gingerly touch the back of his head. He winced, his fingers coming away covered in blood.

"You bitch," he said, without much rancor, too stunned to work up a good mad yet.

"You're getting blood on my floor, Errol Wilson," Lila said as she snapped off the safety and pointed the gun at his head. "If you think I won't kill you right now you are sadly mistaken. Imagine what your wife will say when the sheriff has to tell her that I killed you to keep you from raping me."

"You're going to regret this," he said, but made no move to come at her again as he got to his feet. He wobbled a little as he attempted to button up his shirt. She followed him to the door, the gun on him.

"It won't be my first regret," she said as she watched him drive away.

CARTER HAD BEEN so lost in thought he hadn't realized just how late it was. He'd gone through the items in the evidence bags. A piece of leather, an old notebook, whatever had been written on it faded beyond recognition over the years, a candy wrapper, a package of chewing gum, an assortment of photos of the victim and what he'd been wearing.

The jeans were in good shape. The shirt was so faded it would have been hard to know the exact color. What caught Carter's attention were the man's boots. They were a common brand. The only thing that distinguished them was the color: blue. Dress boots. Same with the man's belt.

Carter inspected the bag containing the marijuana seeds that had been found in the plane, agreeing with Max's drug-smuggling conclusion. Maybe Max was also right that the woman and baby were just cover. Carter couldn't see Nina Mae Cross in that plane, let alone her and a baby. Whose baby? And what about the victim? How did he fit in?

Carter rubbed his eyes and put the photographs back into the evidence bag before locking everything up and heading home.

The box that had been there on his steps was gone. Nor was there any new surprise package waiting for him as he stopped in front of his house. No sign of Deena. But then he never knew what he might find inside. It wouldn't be the first time she'd gotten in.

He didn't know whether to be relieved or worried. His instincts told him that Deena wouldn't let this go. If anything, she was plotting something big, planning an attack that he wouldn't see coming.

Weary and exhausted, he just wanted to go to bed. He hadn't had dinner, but he didn't care. He wasn't hungry, just tired.

He glanced toward the house again, not in the mood for surprises tonight and unsure whether even the new locks could keep Deena out.

As he started to get out of the SUV, his radio squawked.

"Break-in at Dr. Holloway's," the dispatcher said.

Dr. Holloway's? "I'm on it."

Another squawk. "Deputy Samuelson is on his way as well," the dispatcher said.

EVE HEARD a siren blare in the distance, the sound growing as if the vehicle was headed for the doctor's office building.

She didn't take the time to find out what Bridger Duvall had been doing there. She stumbled out the back door and ran.

It wasn't until she reached her pickup that she dared look back. She couldn't see anyone following her. She didn't stop to make sure. She opened her pickup door, tossed the file onto the seat and slid behind the wheel. Unfortunately, when she'd swung her bag of tools at Bridger Duvall, she'd lost her grip. The last she'd seen the bag it had landed somewhere back in archives.

As she pulled out, she saw a woman at the pay phone down the street and recognized her. Deena Turner Jackson. Eve frowned. Was it possible Deena didn't own a cell phone?

Deena exited the booth without looking her way, climbed into an SUV and drove south, probably headed for the country club. There was usually a live band and Eve had heard that Deena was partying it up, trying to make Carter jealous.

Disgusted with that particular love affair, Eve waited to make sure she and Deena Turner Jackson didn't cross paths again before she, too, headed south, toward Old Town.

Her mind was racing. What had Bridger Duvall been doing in the doctor's office and how did he get in? Was it possible he'd broken in through the front door?

She felt almost virtuous about the fact that she hadn't been the only one breaking into Doc's tonight. Also she'd gotten away from Duvall. Both thoughts shocked her. She'd struck the man, knocked him down the stairs, possibly even hurt him. How far was she willing to go to learn the truth? Obviously further than the law allowed.

CARTER HEADED down the street toward the doctor's office building, but at Central he passed a pickup truck he recognized.

Eve Bailey.

She didn't seem to notice him as she drove out of Whitehorse, headed no doubt home.

A break-in at Doc's and Eve Bailey just happens by this late? But why would Eve break into the doctor's office? She wouldn't. Or would she?

He drove to Doc's. Deputy Samuelson was already there. "What's up?"

"Looks like someone broke in not just through the back door but the front," Samuelson said.

"Any idea what they were after?"

"There's a box of files on the floor in the archives room. I'd assume that was what they were looking for."

Carter followed him downstairs to where a large box sat in the middle of one of the aisles, a stool nearby and a crowbar, hammer and screwdriver in a shopping bag next to it.

"Not exactly a professional job," he commented after seeing the broken locks.

He knelt down to take a look at the date on the box on the floor. February 1975.

The year and month Eve was born and which the plane had crashed in the Breaks.

"Anything else disturbed?" he asked.

Samuelson shook his head. "Looks like whatever was in the box is what the burglar came in for."

Carter nodded. "Give Doc a call, then secure the building as best you can."

Outside, he climbed into his patrol SUV and headed south. It was time to have another heart-to-heart with Eve Bailey.

EVE TOOK A BACK road home. As she drove, she watched her rearview mirror. No car came racing after her. But she still had the feeling she was being followed. Didn't most criminals think that?

She was so busy watching her rearview mirror that she was shocked to look up and see a set of headlights coming at her. She swerved back to her side of the road as a pickup blew past going in the direction of town. Eve only got a glimpse of it, but she would have sworn it was Errol Wilson behind the wheel of his old blue rattletrap.

So he hadn't gone to Great Falls with her

mother. But that didn't mean he wasn't headed that way now.

She shoved him out of her mind, still shaking from what she'd done tonight. What had she been thinking?

She reminded herself that she'd found what she'd been looking for. She was adopted, just as she'd suspected. The file proved it. And that, while maybe not making her actions right, allowed her to feel somewhat justified.

Everyone had lied to her. Not that it made any sense. There was no stigma connected to adoption. Why not just tell Eve the truth when she was young? Or when she'd asked?

Because there were other people involved in the deception. The thought made her heart race. Doc, for sure, since he'd signed her birth certificate. But were there others? There would have to be. Like her grandmother and other people in Whitehorse and Old Town who would have noticed Lila Bailey wasn't pregnant, but then had a baby.

Unless her mother had pretended to be pregnant.

Eve rubbed her temple as she drove, her head aching.

Whatever the circumstance of her birth, it had obviously been a well-kept secret. And that worried Eve more than she wanted to admit as she noticed a set of headlights behind her.

The night was pitch-black, the road narrow and dark. Eve watched the headlights behind her, surprised to find anyone else on the road tonight, given the hour.

She told herself that it couldn't be anyone after her. Not this long after the break-in. But still she felt a little spooked. Just nerves. Given what she'd learned lately, who could blame her?

She'd driven this same five miles hundreds of times, but tonight seemed different. Tonight she knew the truth. She was adopted. There was no other explanation. And once she showed her mother the medical file, Lila Bailey couldn't deny it any longer. Eve finally had proof, she thought, glancing over at the file on the seat next to her, then at the headlights behind her.

Eve pressed down on the gas, driving faster, anxious to reach the ranch.

The vehicle behind her stayed back some distance. She could see the headlights in the cloud of dust her tires were kicking up. What had made her think it had been chasing her? Guilt, no doubt.

She tried to relax, but she knew she wouldn't be able to until she'd talked to her mother. And Dr. Holloway.

If she'd known where her mother might be staying in Great Falls, Eve would have gone there. As it was, she'd have to wait until her mother returned from the funeral. If there was even a funeral.

Her mother couldn't stay away forever.

Ahead, the road made a sharp turn to the left, then back to the right. Just a little farther and the back road would connect with the smoother and wider main gravel road into Old Town.

Eve came around the corner as the moon peeked out of the clouds, illuminating the landscape. She caught the glint of something up on the hill ahead of her just an instant before she heard a loud crack, then another. The front tire on the pickup blew.

Eve fought to keep control of the truck, but it was impossible. The rear end came around, the tires burying down into the loose earth at the edge of the road. The pickup keeled hard to the right and rolled, skidding on its top before coming to a stop in the ditch below the road.

Dazed, Eve hung upside down, the seat belt cutting into her. The airbag had deployed, but was now hanging slack in her face.

At first she couldn't move, could barely breathe. Was she all right? She wasn't sure.

She reached for the seat-belt release as the cab suddenly filled with light from the car that had been behind her. She heard the vehicle's engine as it roared toward her.

Where had the shots come from? She couldn't be sure. She'd thought it was someone on the hillside in front of her but it could have been from the vehicle behind her.

Frantically, she hit the seat-belt button, tumbling onto the headliner as the belt suddenly released. She fumbled for the door handle, still disoriented and shaken, confused over what had happened. Had those even really been gunshots?

The door wouldn't open. She swung around and tried the other one, aware that the vehicle had stopped. She heard a door open and close. The slim bright beam of a flashlight flickered across the landscape, headed in her direction.

Was he coming to finish the job?

She grabbed the other door handle but, like

the first, it was jammed. Part of the windshield lay on the ground. Panicked, she kicked the rest of it out, her pulse deafening in her ears, and scrambled out ready to run for her life.

"Eve!"

She stumbled and fell. The beam of the flashlight splashed over her.

"Oh, my God, Eve," Carter said as he dropped to his knees beside her. From up the road came the sound of an engine revving as it raced away, disappearing into the darkness. "You're bleeding. Don't move."

Chapter Thirteen

As Carter brought the patrol car to a skidding halt outside the emergency entrance to the hospital, Eve sat up a little. Her head ached and so did her arm from holding a cloth on the cut over her left eye to stop the bleeding.

Dr. Holloway's big black car was parked in the nearly empty lot. Next to it was Errol Wilson's beat-up blue pickup.

Carter rushed around to her side of the car as she got out and shoved open the emergency entrance door to help her inside.

She saw Errol sitting on one of the exam tables, the curtains surrounding it standing open. Doc had Errol holding a thick piece of gauze on the back of his head. The two had been talking. Not talking, Eve amended. Arguing.

Both Doc and Errol glanced over at the sound of the buzzer announcing an E.R. arrival.

"Take her into the empty examining room down there," Doc said, as he finished putting a bandage on the back of Errol's head.

"I'm fine," Eve told Carter as she climbed onto the examination table.

"I'll be the judge of that," Doc said as he stepped in, going to the sink to wash his hands before he turned to look at her. "Kind of banged yourself up pretty good, young lady." He looked at Carter, hovering beside the exam table. "Help yourself to a soda in that fridge down the hall. I'll take care of her now." Doc closed the curtain as Carter stepped out.

Eve heard the buzzer at the E.R. door as Errol must have left. Under the drawn curtain, she watched Carter's boots as he paced back and forth.

"That cut looks like it might need stitches," Doc said, after he gently pulled her arm down and removed the cloth Carter had had her holding on the cut. He hurried on before she could protest. "I know how you feel about needles, so don't go fainting on me. I might be able to get a butterfly bandage to do the trick if you don't mind a small scar. Yeah, that's what I thought."

Her head was throbbing and she hurt all over, but that pain was nothing compared to her feeling of betrayal. She'd known Doc all her life. He'd patched her up more times than she could remember. She'd trusted and admired him and always believed he'd brought her into this world.

Looking into his kind grandfatherly face, she found it nearly impossible to believe that he was part of the deception.

Every instinct warned her not to confront him. Not until she had the file. But the file was in the wreckage of her pickup. At least she hoped it was still there. What if whoever had shot at her had come back and taken it?

She never would have left the evidence behind, but she hadn't been herself when Carter found her and he hadn't given her time to get anything out of the truck before he'd rushed her to Whitehorse and the hospital.

Eve tried to remain calm, to think. She could use this opportunity. If she was careful. "You know my grandmother," she said, grimacing as he cleaned the wound.

He glanced at her as if worried the cut on her head was more serious than he'd thought. "Nina Mae? Of course I know her."

"I mean, you knew her when she was young. Didn't she date your older brother for a while?"

He kept working and, for a few moments,

she thought he hadn't heard her. "George was far too tame for your grandmother."

She winced as he put pressure on her cut—and remembered the medical file she'd seen earlier in his office basement regarding her grandmother. She felt ice settle in her chest as she remembered that the file had been dated February 7, 1975, the day the plane presumably crashed in the Breaks.

"She broke her leg once, I heard," Eve said, trying to sound as if she was just chatting to keep her mind off the pain. "Didn't you set it after an accident she had?"

He stopped what he was doing to look at her again. "That leg bothering her?"

She had no idea. "I never heard how she broke it." Eve was shaking. So her grandmother really *had* broken her leg. Because of the plane crash?

"Hold still," Doc ordered a little less gently. She felt more pressure over her eye, pain, then he stepped back. "Why the sudden interest?"

She shrugged. "Just curious."

"Sheriff, stop pacing and either sit down or wait outside," Doc snapped irritably.

Eve watched Carter's Western boots disappear from under the curtain, his footfalls disappearing down the hall. "All I remember is

Grandma Nina Mae telling me something about a blizzard?"

Doc gave her an impatient look. "Yes, she went out to check one of the animals, I believe, and fell. Are you sure you're all right?" He was studying her, frowning as he looked into her eyes. "How hard did you hit your head?"

"Not hard. She said it was the same night I was born."

He began putting away his supplies, his back to her. "As I recall, Nina Mae fell on the ice. It was only a hairline fracture. Your grandmother was a strong, determined woman. I just splinted it until she could get into my office."

It all sounded so plausible. If Eve hadn't found the file on her mother's infertility, she wouldn't have noticed that his explanation seemed a little too practiced. She would have believed him.

Also, Doc had given himself away. He hadn't corrected her when she'd mentioned being born the same night her grandmother had broken her leg. She might have been born on February 5, 1975, but according to the file she'd seen in Doc's office, her grandmother had broken her leg on February 7—the same date as that in the crashed plane's logbook.

She knew it didn't constitute evidence. How could Doc remember every birth, every broken leg?

But it made her all the more convinced not only was she adopted but that there was some sort of conspiracy involving her birth and grandmother and the plane crash.

He closed a drawer and turned to look at her. She schooled her expression to one of nothing more than mild interest.

Doc leaned back against the counter, both hands gripping the edge behind him. "Why don't you tell me what this is really about?"

"Sorry, you know me. All this," she said, glancing around the E.R., "makes me nervous."

He studied her. "You should take it easy for a while," he said quietly. "Let your mother see to you."

Let her mother see to her? Eve felt a chill as if the temperature had suddenly dropped in the room. "I'll do that," she lied, shocked by what felt even more like a conspiracy to keep the truth from her.

What had really happened the day the plane crashed in the Breaks? Two days after Eve was allegedly born? One thing was for sure. Her grandmother hadn't been checking animals on the ranch. And a few miles to the south, a man in a small airplane was being murdered. Her grandmother wasn't the only person who'd gotten out of that plane that night. The murderer had been with her.

When Doc led her out of the examination room, Eve realized with a start that he hadn't asked how she'd gotten injured.

CARTER NOTICED that Eve was especially quiet as she came out of the exam room, Doc Holloway behind her, his hand on her shoulder.

"You all right?" Carter asked Eve, worry shooting him to his feet.

"She's going to be fine," Doc said. "She just needs to take it easy."

"We're talking about Eve Bailey, here, Doc," Carter joked, but Eve didn't crack a smile.

"Reminds me of when she was a girl," Doc said. "Always in here for one thing or another. Poison ivy. Broken wrist. Always scraped up and bruised. She just never seems to learn."

Carter saw Eve shiver. He slipped off his jacket and put it around her. She flinched at his touch. He stepped back, giving her space.

"I remember how the two of you used to squabble as kids," Doc said, apparently noticing her reaction. "Didn't she bloody your nose once? Or did she break it?"

"I'd prefer not to go there," Carter joked, but his gaze was on Eve. He was surprised she hadn't jumped into the conversation. It wasn't like her. She was acting strange, no doubt about it. "Thanks for coming down, Doc."

"I had to come down, anyway."

"Yeah, I saw Errol leaving. What happened to him?" Carter asked.

"Working on his tractor, nailed the back of his head good," Doc said. "Glen Whitaker came in before that. Seems he ran off the road. Hit his head. Can't remember what happened."

"He's all right, though?" Carter asked, relieved that Glen had been found and his disappearance apparently solved.

"He'll live," Doc said with a shrug.

Carter noted that Doc hadn't even mentioned the break-in at his office earlier tonight. "Anything missing from your office?"

Doc shook his head. "Probably didn't have time to steal anything, since your deputy said the dispatcher got an anonymous call right away that someone was breaking in. A woman."

"A woman was breaking in?" Carter didn't dare look at Eve.

Doc shook his head again. "No, the call was from a woman. Said she saw someone trying to break in. Too dark to make out who it was. Probably just kids."

Carter wished he believed that.

Eve moved toward the exit, as if anxious to leave this discussion behind. Or maybe just anxious to get home after everything she'd been through.

The cut over her right eye was covered with a white butterfly bandage. She had a baseball-size bruise on her upper left arm from where she must have hit the pickup door and the knee she'd scraped falling into the ravine only the day earlier was bleeding through her jeans.

On top of that, she was still limping a little from her hurt ankle. The woman was a mess. And yet, he thought, he'd never seen her more beautiful.

Doc's cell phone rang on his hip. He excused himself, saying over his shoulder, "Eve, remember what I told you. No more foolishness."

Carter glanced at Eve. What was that about? He recalled overhearing her ask about her grandmother's broken leg. Seemed strange unless you knew that Eve believed her grandmother had been on the plane that crashed in the Breaks February 7, 1975. Carter took her arm as she started to slump. "Let's get you home."

Eve said nothing as he led her outside.

Once in the car, Carter said, "Okay, what's going on? Is it something to do with your accident?" She'd scared him when he'd seen her pickup's headlights and realized that she'd lost control of her pickup…just as she was scaring him now because she'd acted almost as if she was afraid of Doc.

"It wasn't an *accident*," she said without looking at him.

"What?"

"Could we get out of here," she said, as Dr. Holloway came out of the building and looked in their direction.

Carter started the engine, backed out and headed south out of town. "What wasn't an accident?"

"Someone shot out the front tire on my pickup."

He darted a look at her. She wasn't serious. If what she was saying was true, wouldn't she have said something on the way into town earlier? He recalled that she'd seemed to be in shock on the way into the hospital.

He'd heard a vehicle taking off up the road but it hadn't registered at the time that the driver might be somehow involved in Eve's wreck.

Once he'd seen how badly Eve was bleeding, all he'd thought about was getting her to the hospital.

And why would anyone want to shoot out her tire? She had to be mistaken.

"Sometimes a blowout can sound like a gunshot," he said, hoping to hell that was all it was.

"Do two gunshots sound like a blowout?" she asked, glaring over at him.

"Why would someone shoot at you?" He was trying to remain calm, trying to be the sheriff and not her former boyfriend—and lover, even if it had only been that one night.

"You tell me, Sheriff. Couldn't have anything to do with what I found on that airplane, right?"

He preferred her sarcasm over the terrified look he'd seen when she'd come half crawling, half falling, out of her wrecked pickup. Or the odd way she'd been acting around Dr. Holloway.

"Did Doc say something to upset you?" he asked, trying to figure out what was going on with her.

She shook her head and looked away.

"I'm taking you home, then I'll check your pickup."

"No. Stop on the way. There's something I need to get out of the truck."

"Eve, you really need to—"

"I really need to stop at the pickup."

"Fine. I'll stop on the way." He had a bad feeling about what she wanted out of her pickup. The last thing he wanted to do was have to arrest her for breaking and entering before the night was over.

EVE LEANED BACK against the seat, closed her eyes and pretended to sleep. She needed that file. If it was still in the pickup. And she was going to have to tell Carter about it. No getting around that.

As he drove, she considered her actions of the past forty-eight hours and winced inwardly. She'd gone from tampering with a crime scene and withholding evidence to breaking and entering and stealing personal medical records. She'd come home determined to get to the truth. She'd always felt there was a mystery to her birth, but now she suspected it was much more than the fact that she was obviously adopted. A man had been murdered in that plane. And now someone seemed determined to keep her from finding out the truth.

"If there's anything you want to tell me…" Carter said.

She opened one eye to look at him, then closed it.

"Fine."

A thought struck her and she opened her eyes and sat up. Doc said a *woman* made the anonymous call to the sheriff's department about the break-in. That would explain why the woman hadn't used her cell phone. Everyone had cell phones, even though most of them worked only in a five-mile radius around Whitehorse.

So what had Deena been doing on that pay phone down the block from Doc's office? Calling the sheriff's department? Eve felt a chill. Had Deena been following her?

"Something wrong?" Carter asked.

She shook her head, leaned back and closed her eyes again, not wanting to talk. Her head was reeling. She didn't really believe that Deena had nothing better to do than follow her around, did she?

"Are you sure this item you need to get out of your truck isn't something that could wait until morning?" Carter asked as they neared her wrecked pickup lying in the ditch.

She opened her eyes again to glance over at him. He sounded worried. Almost as if he already suspected what she had to get from the truck.

"How did you just happen to come up on me after my pickup went off the road?" she asked.

He cut a look at her. "You don't think I shot out your tire, do you?"

"I thought you didn't believe that."

He groaned. "I saw you leaving town," he said as he turned off the road. "I'd been worried about you."

The patrol SUV's headlights illuminated her pickup. She was shocked to see how badly the truck had been damaged. To realize how lucky she was to be alive.

CARTER FELT a shaft of cold move through him as he saw Eve's wrecked pickup in the headlights. She opened her door and hopped out before he even came to a full stop. He could tell she wasn't steady on her feet. Not that it slowed her.

"Hold on," he called after her. He left the patrol car running, headlights on, and, taking his spare flashlight, went after her.

In the glow of the headlamps, he saw Eve going through the wreckage for something that had apparently been in the cab.

"Here," he said, handing her the spare flashlight.

"Thanks," she said. He saw her shiver as she looked at her destroyed truck.

The way she'd been bleeding, he hated to think what would have happened if he hadn't followed her. Let alone if someone really had shot out her tire.

He reminded himself that the only reason he'd followed her was because he suspected she'd just broken into Doc's office. Actually, he was pretty sure she had. But for the life of him, he couldn't imagine why. Unless it had something to do with her grandmother. Is that why she'd been questioning Doc about Nina Mae's broken leg?

He unhooked his flashlight from his belt and turned it on. "You say the front tire blew?"

"Right front," she said, stooping down to shine her light into the cab. "And it was *shot* out."

He was still hoping she was wrong as he left her to search for what she was looking for while he went to inspect the right front tire. It definitely had blown. There wasn't much left of it. He was thinking he wouldn't be able to tell what had caused the blowout when he saw the dent in the rim.

He let out a curse as he stuck the end of his finger into the hole a bullet had made. Son of a bitch. Eve was right. Given the size of the dent, he would guess the shot had come from a high-powered rifle at some distance away.

When he looked up, he saw Eve crawling out of the demolished cab of her pickup. She had what appeared to be a file folder in her hand. Oh, hell.

"Unless you want me to arrest you for breaking and entering and destroying personal property, you'd better have a good reason for having that file, Eve Bailey."

"I'm adopted," she blurted out, and headed for his patrol car.

"What are you talking about?" he demanded, following her. She had climbed in and was sitting in the passenger seat, the file folder on her lap, her hands on top of it as if she thought he'd try to take it from her.

He slid behind the wheel.

She stared straight ahead and said, "My whole life I've known there was some secret that had to do with me." He heard the catch in her throat. "Just as I've known that I didn't fit in with my family. It isn't just that I don't look like my parents or my sisters. I've always felt…different, incomplete. I know there is a family that I belong to. People who look like me, who have the same smile, the same color hair, the same genes." She stopped to take a ragged breath. "The same medical history."

He could see how upset she was. He'd never dreamed she felt this way. "Why didn't you tell me this when we were—" he was going to say *dating* "—in high school?"

She shook her head. "My mother swore I was just being silly." She looked over at him. "I couldn't understand where these feelings came from. All I knew was that I felt restless. It's why I came back home. I thought maybe I could come to terms with whatever this was that has haunted me all these years. I have to know who I am, can you understand that?"

He couldn't really. He'd always known who he was, although there'd been plenty of times he wished he wasn't a Jackson. But he could see how much this meant to her, how much she needed the truth. And wanting to get to the truth was definitely something he understood.

"This," she said, holding up the file, "proves that I was right. My mother went to Dr. Holloway to discuss *infertility* days before I was born. A woman nine months pregnant isn't worried about being infertile. There is no way Lila Bailey gave birth to me on February fifth, 1975, like it says on my birth certificate. Doc Holloway lied and so did my mother and my father and my grandmother."

"Do you hear what you're saying? That there was a conspiracy to keep you from knowing you were adopted?"

"That's why it never made any sense," Eve said excitedly. "Don't you see? The secret wasn't kept because I was adopted. It was because of the murdered man in the plane in the Breaks. I saw a file in Doc's office on my grandmother. Did you know she broke her leg the same day the plane went down? The same day my grandmother was on that plane."

Carter went deathly still as he thought of the baby brush that the crime techs had found in the plane. "Mind if I see that?" he asked, reaching for the file on her lap.

With obvious reluctance she handed it to him. He turned on the dome light and flipped through the doctor's records, stopping on her mother's doctor visit for infertility.

He looked up at her, his mind on the downlike dark hair in the bristles of the baby brush.

It was all supposition. If her grandmother had been onboard that plane, if there really had been a baby on the plane, if they had both survived…

He let out a curse as he handed back the file. February 7, 1975—the night Doc treated Nina Mae Cross for a broken leg. Two days after the night Eve was said to have been born at the ranch.

He hesitated, then reminded himself that someone had shot out the front tire on her pickup. He had to be honest with her. He could see how determined she was to learn the truth and knew her well enough to realize she wasn't going to stop until she did.

"There's something you should know," he said. "There's a good chance that the day the plane went down, there was a baby onboard."

Eve's eyes filled with tears. "Oh, my God, you think I could be that baby?"

"Eve, let's not leap to any conclusions—without evidence," Carter said quickly as he neared her house.

"But there's a way to find out, right?"

He nodded. "The crime lab took some of the hair from the baby brush found in the plane. If we send them some of your DNA—"

"Then let's do it. If you send it right away—"

"First thing in the morning. I'll put a rush on it."

EVE SAT BACK. Her heart was pounding. But the excitement waned quickly. All the DNA test would do was tell her whether or not she'd been on that plane. She still wouldn't know who she was. Worse, she and her grandmother were somehow connected to a murder.

Carter parked in front of her grandmother's house. Her house, she thought protectively. The sky had already begun to lighten to the east. It wouldn't be long before daybreak. He sounded as tired as she felt.

"Are you sure about this?" he asked quietly. "I just don't want to see you get hurt."

"I've already been hurt. I've been lied to and deceived. You don't know what it's like to be betrayed by the people who are supposed to love you." She stopped, realizing what she'd said. "Or maybe you do."

"Deena," he said like a curse. "She deceived me even *before* we got married."

She'd heard from a friend that Deena had lied about being pregnant to get Carter to marry her, but Eve had thought her friend was just trying to make her feel better about his elopement.

"Once you've done something that you regret," Carter said, "it's often hard to admit how wrong you were. You know you can't undo the damage you've done," he said, looking over at her. "And no matter what you do, someone is going to get hurt."

She saw the pain in his eyes and was surprised at the effect it had on her. She looked away, not wanting to feel any sympathy for him. He'd made love to her for the first time that night, the first time for both of them. Then he'd gone to Deena. If he now lived to regret it, then he'd gotten his just rewards.

"Eve," he said gently. "I've never forgiven myself for what I did to you. I'm sorry. I can't tell you how much I've regretted it and wished—"

She turned toward him, planning to tell him she hadn't given the past—let alone him—a second thought. It was the look in his eyes that stopped her.

"When I saw your pickup tonight upside down by the road and I thought that I might never get the chance to tell you how I feel, how I've always felt…"

She told herself she didn't want to hear this. That she'd never dreamed of a day he would say these words to her.

He dragged her to him, his mouth dropping to hers. Wrapped in his arms after so many years, she lost herself in his kiss. It felt so right.

After everything she'd been through, she just wanted the safety of his arms, to lose herself in his kisses, in his caresses.

Something hit the windshield, making them jump apart. The windshield was covered with what appeared to be dirt and crushed flower petals.

"What the hell?" Carter said, hurriedly getting out of the car.

Eve followed, spotting a dark figure disappearing over the rise in the road. An empty flowerpot lay beside the patrol car. She recognized it as the one that had been on her porch. The porch was empty. Past it, her front door stood open.

She ran toward the house, afraid of what she would find inside. Out of the corner of her eye, she saw Carter hesitate, torn no doubt from going after the person or staying with Eve.

"Eve, wait!" Carter called.

As she rushed to her front door and flicked on a light, she heard a vehicle engine in the distance. She caught her breath as her eyes adjusted to the light. She'd expected the place to be trashed after what the intruder had done with her flowerpot.

To her surprise, nothing looked out of place.

She rushed upstairs, Carter hurrying after her, and stopped in the middle of her bedroom. Everything looked the same.

She stepped to a dresser drawer and opened it.

"Someone went through my things," she said, turning to look at him.

"Deena," he said, and swore. "I only got a glimpse of her, but the flowerpot incident is so like her."

Deena had seen the two of them kissing. Eve groaned inwardly. She had enough problems without Deena.

As she started to turn from the bedroom, she caught a familiar scent. Aftershave. She recognized the smell from her close encounter at Doc's office.

"Deena wasn't the only one who's been here." But why would Bridger Duvall have been in her bedroom?

Chapter Fourteen

"Bridger Duvall?" Carter echoed when Eve told him. "Let me guess. There's more to the story."

"I wasn't alone tonight in Doc's office," she said. "I heard someone else breaking in."

Carter recalled that both the front and back doors at the doctor's office had been broken into. "Are you telling me—"

"Bridger Duvall was there."

"The man who's renting the old McAllister place?"

She nodded.

"Did he see you?"

"He tried to stop me from leaving, but I got away. I'd seen him earlier. Coming out of my grandmother's room at the nursing home. I think he might have taken a photograph of me and my grandmother. It was a baby photograph of me."

Carter swore. "What would he want with a baby photograph of you?"

She shook her head.

"I need to talk to Duvall, but I'm not leaving you here alone," he said, reaching for the phone.

"Who are you calling?"

"Deputy Samuelson. I'll have him come out and stay with you until I get back."

"That isn't necessary." She stuffed her hands in the front pockets of her jeans, putting up a fight, but not much of one. She was obviously frightened after everything that had happened. "I'm fine. You scared off Deena and whoever else was here. I really doubt they'd be foolish enough to come back."

"Someone shot out your tire tonight."

"Probably just a case of mistaken identity."

"Right. We have no way of knowing who was behind it at this point since apparently you've been doing some investigating on your own. I should lock you up for breaking into Doc's office."

She held out her hands for him to put the cuffs on.

"I'm serious, Eve. You've apparently got someone running scared."

She nodded as she put her hands back in her pockets. "Which means it has something to do with me and the plane crash."

"Maybe." He worried it was Deena. "You're in danger and until we find out from whom..."

"I'll start locking my doors and being careful," she promised.

"Right." He called the deputy and hung up. "Samuelson's on his way. He was on a call so he's not far from here." Still, Carter didn't like letting Eve out of his sight. But he knew that wasn't possible, short of arresting her. "Don't give the poor guy a hard time, okay?"

She smiled and he was reminded of their interrupted kiss.

"You should get some sleep."

She nodded, her gaze meeting his, her eyes filling with tears. "What's going on, Carter?" she asked, her voice a hoarse whisper.

"I don't know." He stepped toward her, wanting nothing more than to take her in his arms and comfort her. She'd been through so much.

At first she didn't resist. She felt so right in his arms. She buried her face in his shirt. He pulled her closer. All those old feelings and desires sparked and caught fire.

He remembered their night together in the front seat of his old pickup. He'd never wanted a woman more than he wanted her right now. But he knew that the worst thing he could do was repeat the past. He drew back, holding her at arm's length.

"I can't do this," he said softly.

She shook her head, hurt and anger in her eyes. "What is it you want from me?" she demanded.

"Nothing. That is—"

"No." She stepped away from him. "That's your problem, isn't it, Jackson. You've never known what you wanted."

"You're wrong about that," he said, surprised by her outburst.

"Well, you had your chance. You blew it."

"I know."

"So don't even…" She looked close to tears.

"I want another chance with you, Eve," he said, his heart in his throat. "If you can ever find it in your heart to forgive me. I want your trust. Your love." He took a breath and let it out as he stepped to her, his fingers going to her cheek.

She seemed to hold her breath as he brushed the tip of a finger along her jawline, across her full lips. He heard the small intake of breath she made even over the pounding of his own pulse. "There's always been something between us. Tell me I'm wrong about that."

She said nothing, just looked up at him, her eyes full.

"Only this time, Eve Bailey," he said, drawing back his touch, "I won't be making love to you until our wedding night."

Tears welled to bursting in her eyes. She brushed hastily at them. "You're presuming a lot, Mr. Jackson."

"No, I'm just hoping for a second chance," he said, his voice raw with emotion. "That if you ever need me—"

The sound of a vehicle coming up the driveway drew their attentions. "Samuelson is here," he said.

She nodded.

"Get some rest. I'll be back soon." He headed for the door.

"Carter?"

He turned at the door to look back at her.

"Be careful."

THE SUN WAS JUST CRESTING the horizon as Eve watched Carter go down her porch steps to talk to Deputy Samuelson.

Earlier, all she'd thought about was lying down. She'd felt dead on her feet, emotionally and physically exhausted from the past forty-eight hours.

But now, as she stood watching Carter from the window, all she could think about was the future and what it might hold. She thought of what he'd said.

If she ever needed him? She'd never needed or wanted anyone but him.

Deena would try to make things impossible for them. But Eve knew it wasn't Deena she worried about. It was her own fear of falling for Carter again that gave her pause.

A second chance? Was it possible for them? Eve hated to even hope and yet it was hope that gave her strength right now.

Her stomach growled. She tried to remember the last time she'd had anything to eat. She knew she needed sleep. But the sun was coming up and she had so much on her mind…

She wandered into the kitchen as she heard Carter's patrol car start up. She opened the refrigerator as she listened to him drive away and felt niggling worry at the thought of him confronting Bridger Duvall.

As she pulled out the ham, cheese and eggs she'd bought at the store, she wondered if Deputy Samuelson would want some breakfast.

She hadn't heard his tread on the porch. As she started to turn to look out through the living room to see if he was still in his car, she heard the creak of a floorboard behind her an instant before a hand cupped her mouth.

The dozen eggs fell to the floor, followed by the package of sliced ham and cheese. Eve struggled to fight off her attacker, but he was larger and stronger, as he dragged her out the back door and across the yard toward the barn.

CARTER PARKED his patrol car in front of the old McAllister place and got out. The large sprawling ranch house sat silent in the early-morning light.

He'd heard the place had been sold to a former stock detective and her husband. Apparently, Bridger Duvall was renting it in the interim. Carter hadn't been able to learn much about Duvall on his way out to the house.

Duvall was single, had lived in Bozeman, about five hours to the southwest, and had been a chef at a couple of restaurants. He was thirty-two and had no warrants or arrests on his record.

Carter didn't see Duvall's black car as he walked up the steps to the front door, rang the bell and waited. A barn cat ambled across the yard, eyeing him distrustfully. In the tall grass crickets chirped. The air was heating up fast, the scents of clover and hay strong. It was going to be another hot one. Which probably meant another afternoon storm.

Carter tried the bell again, then knocked. Still no answer. Walking over to the garage, he cupped his hands over his eyes and peered in. Empty. Either Duvall hadn't come home last night or he'd taken off early this morning.

The sheriff hesitated, then went back to the front door and tried the knob. Few people locked their doors in this part of Montana, but Duvall wasn't from here. To Carter's surprise, the door swung open.

Any evidence he found would be inadmissible in court, he told himself as he stepped inside. But after what Eve had told him about Duvall breaking into Doc's office building last night and possibly being in her house tonight, Carter wasn't about to leave until he looked around.

"Anyone home?" he called.

He wasn't expecting an answer and he didn't get one. He moved through the house. The air was cool and a little stale. He got the impression Bridger Duvall didn't spend much time here. What bothered Carter was what Duvall was doing here in the first place? It certainly was no vacation destination. Few people had ever heard of Whitehorse or Old Town.

Moving through the house, Carter saw that there were no personal items in the living room, kitchen or dining room. Three of the bedrooms were completely empty. The fourth had a bed, the blankets on it crumpled.

Carter stepped in. There was a half-empty water glass next to the bed. He moved around to the other side. A book lay on the floor. A mystery, one Carter had been meaning to read.

Nothing here of any interest. He felt relieved, although he had no idea what he'd expected to find.

As he turned to leave, he saw the back of the bedroom door. A cheap cork bulletin board had been tacked to it. The bulletin board held a half-dozen snapshots.

Carter stepped closer. His heart began to pound. The photographs were of Eve Bailey, all candid shots taken with a wide-angle lens from a distance. And one of her as a baby with her grandmother.

There were photographs of her going into

the Whitehorse rest home, ones of her coming out of the grocery store, another of her getting gas at Packy's on the way out of town.

But it was the photograph of Eve saddling up her horse next to the barn and another of her painting late at night inside her grandmother's house that struck like a blade through the heart.

He tried his cell. No service. He rushed out of the house to his patrol car and grabbed his radio. Deputy Samuelson didn't answer. Carter told himself that the deputy was probably in the house with Eve. Knowing her, she was probably making him breakfast.

But he couldn't shake the feeling that Eve was in terrible trouble as he leaped into his car, started the engine and took off in the direction of her house.

A mile up the road, his radio squawked. He snatched it up, praying it was Samuelson. It was the dispatcher with an urgent call from Max Roswell at the crime lab.

"Patch him through." Carter held his breath as he heard Max's voice.

"We've identified your vic from the plane," Max said. "We got lucky. He had a variety of tattoos. One with his military unit number. Another of a heart with two names inside, his and a woman's. Even with the skin mummified we were able to enhance both tattoos by using a computer program. This high-tech stuff is truly amazing."

Carter could have cared less how they'd done it. "Who is he?"

"You might know him," Max said. "He dropped off the radar screen thirty-two years ago. Name's Charley Cross. The woman's name on the tattoo is Nina Mae."

Eve's *grandfather* was the victim?

"You still with me?" Max asked. "I take it you know him?"

"Yeah," Carter managed to say. "He supposedly ran off thirty-two years ago. To Mexico. At least that was the rumor." He recalled how devastated Nina Mae had been after that.

"He didn't get quite that far," Max said.

Carter's mind was reeling. No wonder Nina Mae had been devastated. If she and Charley had been on that plane…

"By the way," Max was saying. "Those hair samples we took from the baby brush. We ran a couple of DNA tests. The hair was from two different babies. But are you ready for this? They were related."

EVE FOUGHT as hard as she could while being dragged into the dark barn. She could tell by his strength that he was a man. The perspiration smell of him made her nauseous.

Swearing as she connected the heel of her boot with his shin, he threw her down hard. It took her breath away, but she scrambled to her feet, ready to run.

Errol Wilson blocked her escape. He had pulled a gun and now held it on her. "I told your mother to do something about you or I would."

She felt the nausea rise in her throat. "What did my mother ever see in you?" she demanded angrily.

"The bitch did this to me," he said, gingerly touching the bandage on the back of his head with his free hand. "I warned her she'd be sorry. She thought she could string me along, paying me off with money, holding back what I really wanted."

A light burned in his eyes. Eve saw both lust and hate. "You weren't lovers." She couldn't believe the sense of relief she felt.

"Your mother is one coldhearted bitch," Errol said angrily. "I told her she'd regret it. But then she never knew what was at stake. She was so busy trying to protect everyone else." He smiled smugly. "Come on." He motioned to the back of the barn. "I have a little present for you."

Eve glanced into the cool darkness, afraid of what he planned to do. "Why don't you tell me what it was my mother didn't get."

He sneered at her. "You've been watching too many of those shows on television. If you think you can distract me by getting me to talk, think again." He motioned once more with the gun. "I can kill you here if you like, but then you'll never see your surprise. It's waiting for you in the car just outside."

Carter. It was her first thought. "What did you do with the deputy?"

"He won't be saving you. If you know what I mean." Errol laughed. His face quickly turned ugly. "Don't make me tell you again." He pointed toward the back of the barn.

Eve moved slowly, searching the darkness for a weapon. But she saw nothing she could get to fast enough to defend herself before he shot her. She didn't doubt that Errol would shoot her. Probably not to kill. He wanted her to see her surprise first.

Bracing herself, she pushed open the door at the back of the barn and blinked. Bridger Duvall's large black car was parked a few yards away, the trunk open a crack.

Errol shoved her forward, knocking her into the side of the car. He reached into the back seat. "Here," he said, "hold out your hands, wrists together. That's right."

Still holding the gun on her, he awkwardly wrapped the tape around her wrists with his free hand.

"That's too tight. You're cutting off the circulation," she said.

"Boo hoo for you," he said, and ripped the end before tossing the roll into the back again. He lifted the lid of the trunk all the way up.

Eve stared down at Bridger Duvall curled in the large trunk. His ankles were taped, his wrists taped behind him. He had a gash on his forehead that had bled but stopped. His eyes were wide. Scared. Just like her.

"Get in," Errol ordered.

Eve reared back. She hated cramped spaces. "Please, don't—"

Errol slapped her across the face. "Get in. Lie down. You cause me any trouble and I'll tape your ankles and your mouth."

He shoved her into the back next to Duvall. "You two make yourselves comfortable. We've got a long ride ahead of us." He slammed the trunk lid.

Eve tried not to scream in the total darkness of the trunk. She couldn't catch her breath.

"Breathe normally," Bridger ordered. "There's plenty of air. Your eyes will adjust and you'll see some light. You're all right."

She wasn't all right. Errol had gone mad. Who knew what he'd done with the deputy Carter had left with her. Or what he planned to do with her and Bridger.

The car rocked. The engine roared. The radio came on as the car began to move.

Bridger was right. She could see light, faint, the opening small. At least they wouldn't die of asphyxiation.

"Who is this guy and what does he want with us?" Bridger asked.

"Errol Wilson. I don't know." She could barely make out Bridger's features even though she was only inches away.

"You all right now?"

No. "As all right as I can be under the circumstances."

"So you're not part of this?" he asked.

Obviously not. "You know what *this* is?"

"Haven't you guessed what you and I have in common? Other than the obvious," he added.

"We're burglars?"

He smiled a little at that, his teeth flashing in the dim light. "We were both looking for files in Dr. Holloway's office. Why is that?"

"You tell me."

"February fifth, 1975." He must have seen her reaction. "The day you were born."

"How do you know that?" The car must have reached the main road. It sped up. Her wrists ached from the tape and her body from the jarring ride.

"I came to Whitehorse looking for you."

His words stunned her. She recalled him coming out of her grandmother's room pocketing a photograph she was sure he'd stolen of her as a baby. Her fear, already off the charts, spiked. "*Me?*"

"What did you find out the other night in the archives?" he asked. "Come on. We don't have much time."

"I found evidence that I was adopted."

"You didn't already know that?" He sounded surprised.

She shook her head, not wanting to admit her mother had lied to her.

"I always knew," he said. "But it wasn't until my adoptive mother was dying that she told me the rest."

She held her breath. "The rest?"

"It wasn't a legal adoption. They knew someone who knew someone, a woman doctor in Great Falls who found babies for couples that were ineligible to adopt for whatever reason. With my mother, it was poor health."

Eve felt her heart begin to pound as she recalled the funeral her mother had gone to yesterday. Could it be the same doctor?

"It was all done in secrecy. The couple would get a call in the middle of the night," he continued. "They'd go to the designated spot and would be given a baby and a birth certificate."

She knew even before he spoke what was coming.

"My parents came to the original White-horse Cemetery the night of February seven, 1975."

Chapter Fifteen

Carter came roaring up next to Deputy Samuelson's patrol car. Through the curtainless windows, he didn't see Eve or Deputy Flynn Samuelson as he jumped out of the SUV and ran toward the house.

Something was wrong. He could feel it as he pounded up the steps and across the porch. He could see into the house, past the living room, something spilled on the floor in the kitchen.

"Eve! Flynn!" he called, as he raced inside. "Eve!"

The house echoed his cries and his footfalls as he dodged paint cans to reach the kitchen.

A pool of broken eggs lay next to the carton. Near it lay a butcher-wrapped package. His attention flew to the empty kitchen and, beyond it, the open back door.

Eve. He was on his phone as he ran out. No

sign of Eve in the yard or the barn. The dispatcher answered on the first ring.

"I need the other deputies out to Old Town Whitehorse right away," he said into the phone. "Eve Bailey and Flynn Samuelson are missing. Tell the deputies to begin a search of the area."

He disconnected, glancing down the road toward the Bailey ranch. Lila's pickup sat out front. Next to it was a rental car. The same color and make as the one his father had been driving.

EVE FELT her heart lodge in her throat as she looked at Bridger Duvall. "You think you were the baby on the plane that crashed in the Breaks?"

"I *know* I was."

She felt her heart drop. She'd been so sure it was her. "How can you know?"

"My mother told me that they got me from an elderly woman at the old Whitehorse, Montana, cemetery the night of February seven, 1975. These women placed babies. The way it worked was that if you wanted a baby you let someone know. Then you'd get a call, often in the middle of the night. You drove to the cemetery."

"The cemetery?" She remembered stories

about strange lights in the cemetery at night, which persisted to this day.

"You waited until someone showed up with a baby and a birth certificate, no questions asked," he continued. "My mother and father desperately wanted a child. They would have done anything." He smiled ruefully at that. "They did. They drove all night to get here and waited in freezing temperatures. And just when they thought they'd been duped, an elderly woman tapped on their window and handed them me and my birth certificate."

Not her grandmother. Someone else. Because Grandma Nina Mae had a broken leg. Was it possible Bridger was wrong about the date? She felt the car slow. Errol turned onto another road, this one paved. The car sped up.

"It was the wrong birth certificate," Bridger said, making Eve start. "The woman had to go back and get the right one. The first one was for a girl, born the same day as me. The name on her birth certificate was Eve Bailey."

Eve began to cry silently. She'd known the moment Carter told her about the possibility of a baby being on that plane that it was her. She'd never imagined, though, that there had been *two* babies.

"Why didn't you come to me with this information?" she demanded.

"Why would I? I had to assume that you knew, that you were in on it. My mother warned me that I might never know the truth because the whole operation was run by a close-knit group of women who, according to the lady Great Falls doctor, planned to take the information to their graves."

She didn't know what to say.

"We look enough alike and, given the fact that we were both brought in on the same night, there's a chance you're my sister."

"That's not possible." She remembered how much her father had wanted a son. Grandma would have known that. She wouldn't have split up a brother and sister. "They wouldn't have split us up."

"My parents had been on the waiting list for years, but they could only afford one child," he said. "We had a small ranch down by Roundup. My father needed a son if he hoped to hang on to it."

She was angry with whoever had done this, but sympathetic to what Bridger's parents must have gone through knowing there was a sister they couldn't take. "Do they still have the ranch?"

"My parents are buried there. Your grandmother was the woman who met my parents that night in the cemetery, wasn't she?"

"No. She *was* on the plane. But she broke her leg that night. She couldn't have been the one. She wouldn't have split us up. Not for any reason."

"Then who? You're from here, you must know."

She shook her head. "It was so long ago, if the woman was elderly, she might be dead by now."

"Someone around here knows. If there was a waiting list then someone has to have kept track of the adoptions, the birth mothers, which families got which kid. There has to be a record. Some proof."

She felt numb. Her mind kept telling her none of this was happening. "Where does Errol Wilson come into all this?"

"I don't know. I've just been trying to find out who I am," he said quietly.

Better to worry about how to find his birth mother than what was going to happen when Errol got them wherever he was taking them, she thought, no matter how futile it might be.

Was it possible they were brother and sister? For so long she'd yearned for someone who looked like her. Bridger Duvall definitely did. Her throat tightened, eyes filling again with tears. A brother? One she might never get to know.

"If, when, we get out of this, I'm going to find her," Bridger said. "And I'm going to find where they recorded the names."

"What they were doing was illegal, why would they keep a record?" she said. "It's been such a well-kept secret I doubt there is any way to prove who was behind it."

"Except there's a murdered man in that plane, right?" he said. "And that's why we're in this trunk. Seems pretty obvious that someone's scared we know too much."

"Who told you about the murdered man?" she asked.

"Errol."

Errol slowed, turned and the road got much rougher.

"I don't understand this," she said. But she doubted it would be long before they found out what he had planned for them.

"I suspect it has something to do with the dead man in the plane," Bridger said. "There's no statute of limitation on murder. What's a couple more murders if there's a chance of covering up the first?"

CARTER'S FATHER LOOKED up in surprise as Carter stormed into the Bailey kitchen. Loren

Jackson sat at the kitchen table. Lila Bailey sat across from him. They both had mugs of coffee in front of them and somber expressions on their faces. A stack of photographs had been pushed to one side.

"Carter?" Loren said in surprise.

"I thought you were at a funeral in Great Falls?" Carter said to Lila, hating the accusation he heard in his voice.

"It was a short sunrise funeral. Only close... friends," she said, as if his storming in was nothing out of the ordinary.

"I need to know what the hell is going on and I need to know right now," Carter said. "Eve's missing. And so is the deputy I left with her."

Lila rose halfway out of her chair. "She's probably taken off into the Breaks again—"

"She didn't go for a horseback ride," Carter snapped, voice rising. "She's in trouble because of that damned plane, because of your lies. I just got the ID on the victim in the plane. It was Charley Cross, your father."

She stood, her hand on the back of the chair shaking. "None of that matters. We have to find Eve and—"

"You knew." Carter swore and looked at his father and saw he, too, knew. He swore again. "All these years the two of you have been covering for a *murderer?*"

"My father wasn't murdered," Lila said. "He was killed in the crash."

"When Eve found the plane, he had a knife sticking out of his chest."

All the blood drained from Lila's face. Loren reached for her, but she shooed him away and lowered herself back into the chair. "Oh, God. I didn't know. I swear I didn't know," Lila said, sounding near tears. "Mother said Daddy died in the plane crash."

"Who was the pilot?" When neither answered, he slammed his fist down on the table, unable to control his anger or his frustration or his fear for Eve. The photographs that had been stacked near the edge started to tumble off. Lila reached for them instinctively. He grabbed them first, spilling them across the table.

"You have to tell me. It's the only hope I have of finding Eve, of stopping this before…" Carter couldn't voice his worst fear. "Who was the *pilot?*"

Lila shook her head, her eyes filled with fear. "I don't know. I swear. The fewer people who knew the specifics the better, so Mother never told me."

"Knew what? Damn it. Tell me what the hell your parents were doing on the plane that night."

"They were bringing in babies. Flying them in," Loren said. "I knew about the babies, but I never flew for them, neither did your grandfather."

Carter stared at him. "I don't believe you."

"I had Cade, and your mother was pregnant with you. I didn't want anything to do with it," Loren said more forcefully.

Why didn't that ring true? And then it hit Carter. "You were afraid if you got caught you would lose your pilot's license. That's all you've ever cared about."

"Not all." Loren glanced across the table at Lila.

Carter turned to Lila. "Your mother just left her husband in the plane?"

"She had to protect the babies," Lila said, her voice thick with emotion. "He was dead. If she told anyone, there would be an investigation. She would never betray the babies. Not even for the man she loved."

"Wait a minute," Carter said. "How many babies are we talking here?"

"Dozens," Loren said, looking at Lila for confirmation. "It started back in the 1930s when the CCC was up here building Fort Peck Dam—all those men turned loose on Montana."

Carter had heard about the red-light district outside of Fort Peck. He had a pretty good idea where some of the babies came from.

"Many of the girls were from good families, even distinguished families," Lila said. "They couldn't keep their babies because they were too young or poor or because their parents wouldn't allow it. With other women desperate for children, someone had to find those babies good homes."

"I thought that's what adoption agencies were for," Carter retorted.

"These were Montana women and men, often with little resources. In my mother's case, it was her age, her economic bracket, the fact that she lived so far from a hospital," Lila said.

Carter stared at her in disbelief. "*You* were one of the babies?"

She nodded. "My mother and father couldn't have children. It was one of the reasons they dedicated their lives to what the circle had started."

"The circle?" he asked, frowning.

"The Whitehorse Sewing Circle," she said. "That's where it began years ago. One of the women heard about a pregnant girl who couldn't keep her baby. The circle decided to help her and made arrangements for the baby to go to a good local family. That's how it started. Later we had the help of several doctors."

Carter stared at her. "That's how you got Eve."

Lila nodded. "And McKenna and Faith."

"They were *adopted,* too?" He raked a hand through his hair and checked his watch. He had to find Eve. "What about the drugs?"

Lila looked at him in surprise.

"The pilot of the plane was smuggling in marijuana along with babies," Carter said.

"That's not possible. My parents never would have—"

He cut her off. "We don't have time for this now. I need to find out who was piloting that plane the night it crashed in the Breaks." He looked to his father. "You let them use our airstrip on the ranch. Don't tell me you didn't know who was behind the controls."

"That was your grandfather's doing. He allowed them to use the airstrip, but he never flew the planes. He made sure none of us was around when a plane was coming in with a…package," Loren said.

Eve had believed there was a conspiracy to keep the truth from her. She had no idea. And Old Town Whitehorse was perfect for this kind of operation. Isolated and close-knit.

"If my father discovered the plane was carrying drugs and that the pilot…" Lila looked up at Carter. "This pilot, he has my daughter?"

"I think there's a good chance," Carter said. "That's why I have to find him." Before he kills again. "I have no idea even where to look."

The circle could have gotten pilots from out of town. Even out of state or out of the country. Canada was less than fifty miles from here. For all he knew the killer could be transporting Eve across the border at this moment. After all, getting into Canada, if you knew the back roads, was just a matter of opening a barbed wire gate and driving through.

He picked up one of the photographs that had spilled across the tabletop, his mind reeling. It was a picture of his father and Lila. They were both very young and, even in the faded photo, Carter could see that they were in love.

Past it was a snapshot of his father and grandfather standing next to Loren's first plane, under it an older black and white of his grandfather's squadron from WWII.

Carter felt a jolt as he reached for it. "You didn't tell me Dr. Holloway flew with Grandpa in WWII."

"Doc got shot down. He never flew again," Loren said.

"At least not that you know of," Carter said as he stared at the photograph of a much younger Dr. Holloway. "He signed all the birth certificates, right?"

Lila nodded.

Next to Doc in the picture was a kid who didn't even look eighteen. He looked vaguely familiar. "Who is—"

"That's Errol Wilson," Loren said. "He was a mechanic at the end of the war. He loved to hang out with the pilots, Dad said. Loved to fly."

"Errol had a *pilot*'s license?" Carter said, remembering the way Errol had been acting around Eve that day in the Breaks.

"No," Loren said. "That is, he had his license, but he got it taken away because of some mess or another he was involved in. Errol never got over it. Worst thing that can happen to a man who loves to fly."

"Errol and Wanda never had any children," Carter said, his mind racing.

"No, Wanda couldn't conceive," Lila said.

Carter felt his heart rate take off at a gallop. "The circle didn't offer them a child?"

Lila met his gaze, hers hard and cold. "Errol didn't want someone else's bastard. There were enough of them in Whitehorse as it was, he said."

Carter hurriedly got on his radio and put out an APB on Errol Wilson. Then he asked Lila where he could find Doc.

"He came back from Great Falls when I did. He said he had work to do. So I assume he's at his office."

Carter's two-way radio squawked. "Sheriff, we found Samuelson."

ERROL BROUGHT the car to a stop and killed the engine, filling the trunk with an eerie silence.

Eve looked at Bridger and saw her own fear mirrored in Bridger's eyes as she heard the car door open, felt Errol climb out. The door slammed. A moment later, she heard the key in the trunk lock.

The lid opened. Eve blinked at the sudden light.

"Come on, you two," Errol said. "We don't have all day."

Past him, Eve saw pine trees. She tried to retrace the trip in her mind, remembering the bumpy roads then the paved, then another rough road to here.

The nearest pines would be in the Breaks. But Errol had driven on paved highway for what had seemed like at least an hour. If he'd gone south… Doc Holloway had a cabin in the Little Rockies near Zortman.

Errol helped her out. Her legs were cramped, her wrists aching from the tape, but she found her feet and glanced around. Doc Holloway's old Suburban was parked in the pines nearby.

Drawing a knife, Errol cut the tape on Bridger's ankles. He sheathed the blade to pull the gun again and pointed it at Eve's head.

"Unless you want to see your twin's head blown off, you won't do anything stupid," Errol said, pulling her back a few feet to give Bridger room to get out.

"So we *are* twins," Bridger said.

"Fraternal, according to Doc," Errol said.

"Doc Holloway? We were born locally?" Eve asked.

"Up north by the border. A home delivery," Errol said.

"What else did Doc tell you about us?" Eve asked. "Do you know who our birth mother was?"

"Doc didn't say, I didn't ask," Errol said. "I had to land on the highway up there. Doc met the plane with the two of you. Whoever your mother was, I'm sure she was just glad to get rid of you."

"You're a real bastard, you know that?" Bridger said.

Errol laughed. "Takes one to know one."

"The sheriff will be looking for us," Eve said.

"Everyone will be looking for you," Errol said. "But they won't find you. Not for a while, anyway. Come on." He shoved her toward a path that led up the hill. "Either of you does anything stupid and I shoot to kill, understand?"

"You're going to kill us, anyway," Bridger said, behind Eve as she started up the trail.

"I can do it now if you keep mouthing off," Errol shot back. "This is your own fault. You just couldn't quit putting your nose into things. You have only yourself to blame."

"Yeah, you keep telling yourself that all the way to hell," Bridger said.

Eve heard Errol hit him from behind. Bridger let out a "whuft" sound. She looked back, afraid of what Errol had done to him, but Bridger motioned for her to keep moving. "I'm fine," he said.

"He tell you that he's been spying on you? I caught him taking pictures of you," Errol said.

Eve turned a little to look back at him.

"Her name was the only one I had. I had to assume she was in on the cover-up," Bridger said.

"Yeah? Well, between the two of you,

you've made a real mess for me to have to clean up," Errol said.

As Eve topped a rise in the trail, she saw the cabin. It was small, built of logs, set back against the mountain. There was a porch across the front and an old rocking chair. Next to it, a creek tumbled in a waterfall to drop a good twenty feet into a rocky pool below.

The roar of the creek reminded her of something Doc Holloway had once told her about his cabin. *"I have an old rocker on my cabin porch. Someday I'm going up there and I'll just sit and listen to the creek next to my cabin instead of whining patients. Someday soon."*

She felt tears rush her eyes. This couldn't be happening. Errol had always scared her. She didn't doubt he planned to kill them. But not Doc. And yet it had been Doc's name on her birth certificate. He was in this up to his neck. But he wouldn't be part of a kidnapping, possibly even murder. She recalled last night at the hospital when she'd seen Errol and Doc arguing. Is this what they'd been arguing about?

As sunlight caught on one of the cabin windows, she told herself Doc wasn't a killer. He was a healer. He had always been kind to her. He wouldn't let Errol kill them. In fact, she was sure Doc would be furious that Errol had brought her and Bridger here. He would fix this, just as he'd fixed her broken wrist when she was eleven.

The cabin door opened.

JUST DOWN THE ROAD from Eve's house, deputies had found Deputy Flynn Samuelson's body stuffed in a ditch culvert. Samuelson had his throat cut.

Eve was still missing.

Trying not to panic, Carter called for the coroner and an ambulance and ordered the deputies to keep searching for Eve. He felt his despair growing. Just as he suspected, a killer had Eve. He feared it was the same one who'd murdered her grandfather thirty-two years ago.

"Sheriff!" one of the deputies called from the barn. "I found something. Better come take a look."

Carter entered the dark barn, his heart in his throat. The deputy was standing by the back door, the sunlight streaming in from outside. *Please, don't let it be Eve.* He moved through the barn, bracing himself for the worst.

"I found tire tracks where a vehicle had been parked back here," the deputy said as he led him outside. "I found this by the back door." He stepped over to the side of the barn. "In the grass."

Carter held his breath as he drew back the high grass. He stared down at the wallet. It was black leather, expensive looking. As shiny as it was, the wallet hadn't been there long.

"I didn't touch it," the deputy said.

"Good work." Carter picked up a stick and carefully opened the wallet to expose a driver's license. Bridger Duvall. What the hell was his wallet doing here?

"Isn't really a place where a man would drop his wallet," the deputy said. "It's almost as if someone threw it into the grass there—"

"So we would find it," Carter finished for him. Was it possible the killer had both Eve and Bridger Duvall? He recalled what Max Roswell from the crime lab had said about the baby hair in the brush found in the plane. Two different individuals. Two babies on the plane. Related to each other.

He checked Bridger Duvall's birth date, knowing even before he looked that it would be February 5, 1975.

His cell phone rang. He jerked it from his hip. "Jackson."

"More trouble, Sheriff," the dispatcher

said. "It's Doc Holloway's office building. It just exploded. They think Doc is trapped inside."

THE CABIN DOORWAY FILLED. Eve felt her mouth go dry as she saw that it wasn't Doc Holloway who stepped out.

"Took you long enough," Wanda Wilson said as she moved aside to let her husband and his kidnap victims enter the cabin. She was a wide-bodied, short woman with a round face, close-set eyes and gray hair. For as long as Eve had known her, Wanda had worn a sour expression, as if she'd just eaten something bitter.

Eve glanced from Wanda to the roar of the creek far below the porch. As she looked down and saw the water rushing over the boulders, she felt a wave of vertigo and stumbled.

"What's wrong with you?" Wanda demanded.

"The tape is cutting off my circulation."

"It won't hurt much longer," the older woman shot back.

Errol stopped for a moment, motioning to everyone to be quiet. Eve heard it, too. The sound of a car coming up the cabin road. Then there was nothing but the wind high in the pines and the chatter of squirrels off in the distance.

"I didn't hear anything," Wanda said. "But let's get this over with and get out of here."

"Why are you doing this?" Eve asked, stopping short of the doorway to look back at Errol. She'd definitely heard a vehicle down the road. She was praying it was Carter. All she had to do was buy her and Bridger time.

Errol jammed the barrel of the gun into Bridger's ribs and she thought for a moment he was going to pull the trigger in answer.

"Because of your grandfather, that righteous son of a bitch," Errol snapped.

"Don't," Wanda warned.

"Why not tell them? You want to know why you both have to die? Because you're just like your grandfather, Charley Cross, that's why. He couldn't keep his nose out of other people's business. Him and his high-and-mighty good deeds."

"Errol—"

He didn't seem to hear as he continued his tirade. "Ol' Charley thought I should just fly bastard babies all over the state out of the goodness of my heart. Oh, sure, he'd pay for plane rentals and fuel, then slip me a twenty like I was some servant. He could have overlooked the weed I was running. The bastard was going to turn me in. After everything I'd done for him and your grandmother."

"Oh, my God," Eve said, her knees giving out.

"Damn it, Errol!" Wanda bellowed as she kept Eve from falling all the way to the porch floor. "Shut the hell up."

"What difference does it make now if she knows I killed her grandfather?" Errol demanded. "Your grandmother thought the plane crash killed him. Charley was unconscious. I waited until your grandmother got out with one of the babies, then I stopped Charley from opening his mouth ever again."

Eve began to cry for the grandfather she'd never gotten to know. She thought of Grandma Nina Mae letting the world believe that Charley had deserted her, run off to Mexico. She felt sick to her stomach. Her grandmother had had to leave Charley in the plane, to keep the secret. To protect Eve and Bridger and the other children.

"You bastard!" Eve cried, lunging at Errol. Wanda jerked her back.

"Do that again and I kill your brother right here and now," Errol threatened.

Bridger let out a chuckle. "You were running drugs and using the baby operation as a front. Sounds like a pretty good deal to me."

Eve didn't believe Bridger for a moment, but Errol did.

He chuckled. "Maybe I was wrong. I should have taken this kid. The kid and I would have had a great business going. We could have cut Doc out of it entirely."

"Doc wouldn't have gotten involved in selling drugs," Eve said, not so sure about that but wanting to believe it was true. She wondered where Doc Holloway was. What if that had been his car she'd heard and not Carter's? What if Errol knew Doc a whole lot better than she did?

"You always were so naive," Wanda said, grabbing her arm and dragging her into the cabin. It was dark inside, only minimal furnishings. Wanda pulled her over to a trapdoor in the wooden floor and shoved her toward the stairs that dropped down into total blackness.

"Don't do this," Eve said. "No one can prove you killed my grandfather. But if you kill me, Carter won't stop until he finds you." It wasn't much of a threat, but once she said it she knew it was true. "He loves me. He's always loved me. He will track you to the ends of the earth."

Wanda laughed. "Yeah, that's why he married Deena Turner."

"Anyway, this isn't my doing," Errol said.

"This is Doc's. His cabin. He's the one who signed all those fraudulent birth certificates. When your sheriff finds the 'retirement' money Doc put away from our drug deals, he won't look any further. He'll believe Doc was flying the plane that night. And there won't be anyone to tell him different."

"Get down there!" Wanda ordered. "Or I'll throw you."

Eve didn't doubt it. She saw no way out. Errol had a gun on Bridger and she suspected it would turn out to be Doc's if Errol had to use it. "At least cut the tape on my wrists. I'm not going to do anything. I know you would shoot my brother if I did."

"Cut the damn tape," Errol snapped. "I'm sick of listening to her whine."

Wanda swore as she took Errol's knife and none too gently cut the tape. "Now get down there."

"What's going on?" asked a voice from the doorway.

Everyone turned at the sound.

Eve stared in disbelief. *"Deena?"*

Chapter Sixteen

Carter raced into Whitehorse. He could see the smoke from miles away. As he approached Dr. Holloway's office building, he saw that it was a total loss.

"Doc?" he asked the chief fireman.

"We got him out. He was in bad shape, but still alive when the ambulance took him to the hospital."

The deputy had reported back that there was no sign of Errol or Wanda at their house. Carter could feel the clock ticking. What if Errol didn't have Eve? What if he was wrong and the killer wasn't local? Eve could be anywhere.

He refused to even consider that she might not still be alive as he drove to the hospital. An internist met him at the door.

"Doc?" Carter asked.

The intern shook his head. "He was too badly burned. Even if we could have gotten him airlifted out to Billings or Salt Lake City to the burn center there…"

Carter rubbed a hand over his face. Doc was gone and so were all the medical records. Also gone was any hope of getting answers.

"He was asking for you right before he died," the intern said. "He kept saying *Sheriff,* and what sounded like *cabin?* Make any sense?"

"Yeah," Carter said, and ran for his patrol car.

EVE WASN'T SURE what Deena saw first, the gun in Errol's hand, the tape binding Bridger Duvall's wrists or the shotgun Wanda had grabbed.

"What's going on?" Deena asked again, her voice breaking as her attention settled on Errol's gun, now pointed at her. "Is this some kind of joke?"

"What are *you* doing here?" Wanda demanded.

Deena seemed to pry her gaze away from the gun to look at the older woman, who had now raised the shotgun, pointing both barrels at Eve and Bridger.

"I was following Bridger's car," Deena

said. "I knew he'd been sneaking around Eve…" She glanced at Eve, then Bridger.

Eve saw that Deena held a small digital camera in her left hand and knew at once what Deena was doing here. She'd planned to expose Eve's affair with Bridger to Carter. The woman was so transparent. She'd seen Bridger following Eve and had followed the two of them—right into trouble.

"What are we going to do with *her?*" Errol demanded.

"What do you think?" Wanda snapped. "We don't have much choice."

Errol started toward the door and Deena. Deena might be transparent and a whole lot more, but she wasn't completely stupid. Sizing up the situation, she turned and ran.

CARTER HAD NEVER been to Doc's cabin, but he knew the small old mining community south of town. And he'd heard Doc talk about the place enough that he didn't have any trouble finding the road.

He parked the patrol car and, taking his shotgun and extra ammunition, sprinted up he road a way before cutting through the trees. He hadn't gone far when he stumbled on a vehicle he recognized. Deena's SUV.

There was a rifle on the floor of the backseat.

"*What the hell?*" Fear threatened to overtake him. Whatever Deena was doing here it couldn't be good.

He could hear the rush of the waterfall even before he topped a rise and spotted the cabin through the trees in the distance. He saw Doc's car was parked below it. And to his surprise, Bridger Duvall's big black car. No sign of Errol's old blue pickup.

Deena and Bridger Duvall?

Doc definitely wasn't inside the cabin. So what was his car doing here?

Cutting through the trees, he circled the cabin, praying he'd come to the right place. Deena's and Bridger's cars being here had thrown him.

As he drew nearer, he heard a gunshot. He began to run toward the cabin, having no idea what he would find once he got there.

THE BULLET ERROL had fired at Deena burrowed into the door frame, the sound booming through the small cabin.

"Get her," Wanda cried, and Errol took off at a run after Deena. Another shot, followed by the splintering of wood and Deena's long eerie cry, then silence.

Even Wanda turned to look toward the porch as if she knew Deena had fallen through the old railing and dropped to the creek below.

Eve saw her chance in that moment when Wanda looked through the open doorway toward the porch. Errol would be back any moment. Eve grabbed for the shotgun.

Wanda Wilson was a strong farm woman. Eve's arms were weak from being bound for so long. She wrestled Wanda for the shotgun knowing she would lose.

Out of the corner of her eye, Eve saw Bridger. He had something gripped in both hands, his wrists still bound. He swung a large stuffed northern pike, catching Wanda in the side of the head. Her grip on the shotgun loosened an instant before she slumped to the floor and Errol yelled from the doorway, "I'm going to kill you sons of bitches!"

Eve would always remember the first shot. It whistled past her ear, so close she could feel its power, hear the rush of the air it filled, smell the gunpowder.

Bridger shoved her aside as Errol took aim again.

"No!" she cried as Bridger lunged at Errol.

She saw Errol swing the gun toward him, the barrel aimed at his chest. She heard the boom. It reverberated through her skull and she screamed again.

The second shot wasn't as loud. Errol seemed surprised by it. In that instant, before Bridger crashed into him, Errol had stood frowning in the doorway staring at Eve as if he'd thought she'd fire the gun.

Errol fell back on the porch as Bridger hit him.

Eve heard another shot and scrambled to her feet, afraid Bridger had been shot a second time.

But Bridger was up, breathing hard, standing over Errol. Next to him, standing in a shaft of sunlight, was Sheriff Carter Jackson. He was still holding his gun, staring down at the dead Errol.

Carter's eyes filled when he saw her. All he had time to do was open his arms as she flew into them.

Chapter Seventeen

When Lila saw Eve, she broke down, ran out into the afternoon rainstorm and threw her arms around her. "I'm so sorry. I'm so sorry."

Eve leaned into her mother. "I'm all right."

Lila pulled herself together, stepping back to hold her at arm's length to study her. "Yes," she said, smiling through her tears. "You're a Bailey. Bailey women are strong. They're survivors."

Eve's eyes filled with tears as she nodded and let Lila take her into the house, leading her to the kitchen.

"Sit here. I'll make you something to eat. You must be starving."

Eve wasn't hungry, but she knew cooking was how her mother had always dealt with every problem, so she said nothing as she watched her.

Lila made a sandwich and slid it in front of her. She looked nervous and afraid to sit down, afraid of what came next.

"We have to talk about it," Eve said.

Lila nodded.

"Do you know who my biological mother is?"

"No." Her mother sank into a chair across from Eve, her hands gripped together on the table. "I never wanted to know. You were a gift, Eve, my first child. I loved you more than life. You were my child, my precious child, a true gift from God."

Eve felt her own tears as she saw her mother's eyes flood. "Why didn't you take Bridger, too?"

She shook her head. "He was promised to the other parents. Chester never forgave me. He always wanted a son. He always said that one reason you felt as if something was missing was because of your twin. I'm sorry, Eve. But I couldn't take that little boy from them. There were other chances to get a son, but by then Chester was too angry to care. McKenna and Faith came to us later." She nodded. "They're adopted, as well."

Eve let that sink in. "Are they sisters?"

Lila shook her head. "No blood relation."

"Do you know who their mothers are?"

"I'm their mother," she said, that iron will in her voice. "Just as I'm your mother. I'm sorry I couldn't tell you that you were adopted when you were young. I realize that was a mistake. You were mine. I never thought of you as belonging to anyone else."

It had begun to rain harder, huge drops splattering against the glass.

"I need to go see Grandma," Eve said.

"I can understand if you're angry with her."

Eve smiled. "I'm not angry." It was true. She was bruised, exhausted, emotionally wrung out, but she wasn't angry or even upset. She'd found out the truth. She didn't want to think at what cost it had come.

She'd discovered a brother she didn't know she had. A deputy had given them a ride back to Old Town Whitehorse while Carter saw that Wanda Wilson was taken into custody and transported to the hospital. Both Deena and Errol would be going to the morgue.

"I want you to know," Bridger had said on the way back. "When I came up here, I wasn't looking to connect with my sister. But I'm glad I found you." He'd sounded as if saying it had come at a cost.

"I'm glad you did, too."

"Even if it almost got us both killed," he'd said with a humorless chuckle. "Would you mind if I stayed around for a while?"

She'd smiled, tears welling in her eyes. "I'd like that."

She knew, though, that part of the reason he was staying in the area was that he hadn't given up on finding their mother. He was convinced that someone here knew the truth. He still hoped to find the woman his parents had met that night in the cemetery.

"I'm all right," Eve told Lila, and smiled as she reached across the table to cover her mother's hand with her own. "Really, Mom."

Tears filled Lila Bailey's eyes. She brushed at them with her free hand. "You'll want milk with your sandwich." She rose to go to the refrigerator.

Eve smiled as she watched her, seeing how hard this was on her, how hard it had been over the years. Lila Bailey *was* her mother. And they were more alike than Eve had ever noticed before, both afraid of showing their emotions, both in love with men who had broken their hearts a long time ago.

She and Lila would never look alike. They didn't share the same blood or the same DNA, but Eve was a Bailey. And somewhere out there was the woman who'd given her and Bridger birth, given them up in hopes they could have a better life. Eve wanted to find her. Not to find herself, because she'd done that right here.

But to thank her.

THE NEXT MORNING, Carter found his father sitting in the Great Northern Café having breakfast. Loren looked up from a back corner table and smiled, rising to his feet to give his son an awkward hug.

"I don't know how you do it," Loren said, motioning to his son to join him. "You want breakfast?"

"Just coffee. Do what?" Carter asked.

"This sheriff thing. You could have been killed yesterday," his father said, his face pained. "You saved Eve's and that other man's life. Is he really her brother?"

Carter nodded. "Not every day is like yesterday." Thank God.

"How is Eve?"

"She's going to be all right," he said, remembering her in his arms. "She's a strong woman."

"Like her mother. I should tell you—"

"You're in love with Lila," Carter said.

"Yes. Chester has agreed to a divorce. The minute she's free I intend to marry her."

Carter nodded, remembering the strained relationship his parents had for years before his mother's death. "Why didn't you marry Lila if you've always loved her?"

"Our story is a little like yours and Eve's. Lila and I were young. We had a fight over what her parents were doing. I got drunk and ended up running into Rachel." He paused. "The next thing I knew your mother was pregnant with Cade. Lila married Chester. I married your mother."

"I always thought it was the flying," Carter said.

"It didn't help," Loren admitted. "Your mother knew about Lila, knew how I felt. I loved your mother. I just couldn't love her enough, if you know what I mean."

"Yes, I do," Carter said, thinking of Deena. "Dad, I wish you and Lila the best. I mean that."

"We'll be going to Florida. Lila wants Eve to have the ranch. She's already talked to McKenna and Faith about it. They were fine with it since neither had planned to come back here after college."

"Does Eve know?" he asked.

Loren nodded. "She told her last night. I take it Eve was very happy. She plans to stay."

Carter poured himself a cup of coffee from the carafe on the table and took a drink to hide how relieved he was. Eve was staying. He hadn't been sure, not after everything that had happened.

The real story about the adoptions hadn't come out. The story around town was that Charley Cross had been flying to the hospital in Billings to visit a friend when the plane went down with Errol Wilson at the controls. Unbeknownst to Charley, Errol had been running drugs.

When Charley realized what was going on, Errol killed him and let everyone believe Charley had run off to Mexico.

Wanda Wilson never stood trial. She was killed by an irate inmate in the Great Falls jail before she could tell anyone about the adoptions or the drug running.

Everyone who knew the truth was either dead or not talking.

Earlier, Bridger Duvall had stopped by his office.

"What are you going to do about the Sewing Circle?" Bridger Duvall had demanded.

"You have any proof?" Carter had asked.

Duvall swore. "You know Eve Bailey and I were on that plane."

The sheriff nodded. "But the pilot is dead. So is Charley Cross and Nina Mae has Alzheimers."

"Lila Bailey knows the truth."

Carter nodded. "But she isn't going to bust some old ladies who made it possible for her to adopt her children. If you're looking for vengeance—"

"Not vengeance, answers. I want to know who my birth mother was and someone in the Whitehorse Sewing Circle knows," Duvall had said angrily.

"Well, no one is talking. If anyone knew, it was Pearl Cavanaugh."

Duvall groaned. "You know damned well that she is incapable of talking since her stroke."

Pearl had a stroke after hearing the news about Errol Wilson's drug running and attempt on Eve's and Bridger Duvall's life.

"Does it matter that much, Bridger? You had parents who loved you. Are you sure you really want to know who gave you birth and under what circumstances?"

"Yes. Eve understands. Did you ask her how she feels about this?" Duvall had asked.

"She's haunted by this, too. You think she is going to let this go?"

Carter hoped she would find peace now that she knew she was adopted, but he feared she had more in common with Bridger Duvall than just being his twin sister.

"I'm going to be sticking around," Duvall had said.

Carter had nodded. "Eve will like that."

"The answer is here," Duvall had said. "I'm not leaving until I find out the truth."

"Son," Loren said now. "You've never taken my advice." His father laughed to soften his words. "But I'm going to give you some advice I hope you'll take to heart. Don't punish yourself the rest of your life for marrying Deena."

He had thought Deena would do that. But now she was dead. Maybe at peace, since she'd never been able to find peace on earth.

Her parents, who had moved to Arizona some years ago, had taken her body to be buried there. Carter had told them that Deena died trying to save Eve and Bridger. It was a small lie, but one that he knew gave them some comfort.

"Don't put off happiness," Loren continued. "Lila and I intend to enjoy what time we have left. Tell Eve how you feel about her."

"I have. It's going to take time, though."

"You have time," his father said, and smiled. "You have the rest of your lives."

Carter finished his coffee and rose from the table. "Eve's over at the nursing home visiting her grandmother. I thought I'd take her to lunch if she's interested. Will I see you later?"

"You'll see a lot more of me. I won't stay away. Lila and I plan to visit often."

"I'm glad to hear that," Carter said. And he was. He'd never seen his father so happy. It looked good on him.

Carter quickened his step. The rain had stopped and he could see a little sun peeking through the clouds. He couldn't wait to see Eve again. Today. Tomorrow. And if he had his way, every day after that.

Epilogue

Charley Cross was buried up on the hill overlooking Old Town Whitehorse one windy hot day at the end of July.

Nina Mae stood at the edge of the grave in her favorite brown coat, wearing the pin Charley had given her. Her back was steel straight, her hands clasped in front of her, her eyes as vacant as the blue sky.

Next to her stood Lila Bailey. She wore all black, including the veil that hid her expression. Like her mother, she stood beside the grave, back ramrod straight.

The entire towns of Whitehorse and Old Town, along with half the county, had gathered for the burial. Eve stood with Carter as Titus Cavanaugh, holding his worn Bible, said what a brave man her grandfather had been, how he had done what he believed to be right and died helping others.

Eve searched the crowd gathered under the summer sun, wondering how many of them had been Whitehorse Sewing Circle babies. She felt an odd sense of peace, knowing she wasn't alone. Knowing what it had cost her grandparents so that she and the others would have homes and parents who loved them.

A part of her knew she would always be looking for the mother who had given her away, searching crowds for a familiar face, listening for a laugh like her own.

Carter squeezed her hand as Titus finished with a prayer.

She squeezed back, happier to have him here than he could know. It would take time, but she knew in her heart that one day they would be together.

As Eve placed a single red rose on the casket, Grandma Nina Mae stepped forward. Lila reached for her, as did several of the mourners.

But Nina Mae only rested her pale hand on the casket, her worn wedding ring glinting in the sunlight. Eve saw tears in her grandmother's eyes as Nina Mae patted the casket, then turned to look at the crowd as if searching for someone.

"Have you seen my granddaughter?" she asked in a trembling voice.

"I'm here, Grandma," Eve said, and took the woman's frail arm.

Her grandmother looked over at her, then placed her hand over Eve's and patted it. "Yes," her grandmother said. "You are here, aren't you?"

* * * * *

THE ROYAL HOUSE OF NIROLI
Always passionate, always proud

**The richest royal family in the world—
united by blood and passion, torn apart by
deceit and desire**

Nestled in the azure blue of the Mediterranean Sea, the majestic island of Niroli has prospered for centuries. The Fierezza men have worn the crown with passion and pride since ancient times. But now, as the king's health declines, and his two sons have been tragically killed, the crown is in jeopardy.

The clock is ticking—a new heir must be found before the king is forced to abdicate. By royal decree the internationally scattered members of the Fierezza family are summoned to claim their destiny. But any person who takes the throne must do so according to The Rules of the Royal House of Niroli. Soon secrets and rivalries emerge as the descendants of this ancient royal line vie for position and power. Only a true Fierezza can become ruler—a person dedicated to their country, their people…and their eternal love!

Each month starting in July 2007,
Harlequin Presents is delighted
to bring you
an exciting installment from
THE ROYAL HOUSE OF NIROLI,
in which you can follow the epic
search for the true Nirolian king.
Eight heirs, eight romances,
eight fantastic stories!

Here's your chance to enjoy a sneak
preview of the first book delivered
to you by royal decree…

FIVE minutes later she was standing immobile in front of the study's window, her original purpose of coming in forgotten, as she stared in shocked horror at the envelope she was holding. Waves of heat followed by icy chill surged through her body. She could hardly see the address now through her blurred vision, but the crest on its left-hand front corner stood out, its *royal* crest, followed by the address: *HRH Prince Marco of Niroli...*

She didn't hear Marco's key in the apartment door, she didn't even hear him calling out her name. Her shock was so great that nothing could penetrate it. It encased her in a kind of bubble, which only concentrated the torment of what she was suffering and branded it on her brain so that it could never be forgotten. It was only finally pierced by the sudden opening of the study door as Marco walked in.

"Welcome home, *Your Highness*. I suppose I ought to curtsy." She waited, praying that he would laugh and tell her that she had got it all wrong, that the envelope she was holding, addressing him as Prince Marco of Niroli, was some silly mistake. But like a tiny candle flame shivering vulnerably in the dark, her hope trembled fearfully. And then the look in Marco's eyes extinguished it as cruelly as a hand placed callously over a dying person's face to stem their last breath.

"Give that to me," he demanded, taking the envelope from her.

"It's too late, Marco," Emily told him brokenly. "I know the truth now…." She dug her teeth in her lower lip to try to force back her own pain.

"You had no right to go through my desk," Marco shot back at her furiously, full of loathing at being caught off guard and forced into a position in which he was in the wrong, making him determined to find something he could accuse Emily of. "I trusted you…."

Emily could hardly believe what she was hearing. "No, you didn't trust me, Marco, and you didn't trust me because you knew that I couldn't trust you. And you knew that because you're a liar, and liars don't trust people because they know that they themselves cannot be trusted." She not only felt sick, she also felt as though she could hardly breathe. "You are Prince Marco of Niroli….

How could you not tell me who you are and still live with me as intimately as we have lived together?" she demanded brokenly.

"Stop being so ridiculously dramatic," Marco demanded fiercely. "You are making too much of the situation."

"*Too much?*" Emily almost screamed the words at him. "When were you going to tell me, Marco? Perhaps you just planned to walk away without telling me anything? After all, what do my feelings matter to you?"

"Of course they matter." Marco stopped her sharply. "And it was in part to protect them, and you, that I decided not to inform you when my grandfather first announced that he intended to step down from the throne and hand it on to me."

"To protect me?" Emily nearly choked on her fury. "Hand on the throne? No wonder you told me when you first took me to bed that all you wanted was sex. You *knew* that was the only kind of relationship there could ever be between us! You *knew* that one day you would be Niroli's king. No doubt you are expected to marry a princess. Is she picked out for you already, your *royal* bride?"

* * * * *

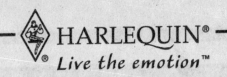

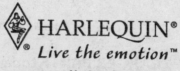

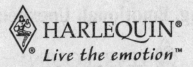

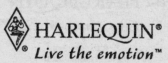

Harlequin® Historical
Historical Romantic Adventure!

*Imagine a time of chivalrous
knights and unconventional ladies,
roguish rakes and impetuous
heiresses, rugged cowboys
and spirited frontierswomen—
these rich and vivid tales will
capture your imagination!*

*Harlequin Historical . . .
they're too good to miss!*

SPECIAL EDITION™

Emotional, compelling stories that capture the intensity of living, loving and creating a family in today's world.

Desire

Modern, passionate reads that are powerful and provocative.

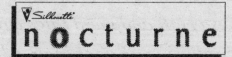

nocturne

Dramatic and sensual tales of paranormal romance.

Romantic SUSPENSE

Romances that are sparked by danger and fueled by passion.

SDIR07